George Dunlop Leslie

Letters to Marco

George Dunlop Leslie

Letters to Marco

ISBN/EAN: 9783744764155

Printed in Europe, USA, Canada, Australia, Japan

Cover: Foto ©Andreas Hilbeck / pixelio.de

More available books at **www.hansebooks.com**

RIVERSIDE, WALLINGFORD.

BY

GEORGE D. LESLIE, R.A.

AUTHOR OF 'OUR RIVER'

London

MACMILLAN AND CO.

AND NEW YORK

1893

PREFACE

THESE letters, which consist chiefly of notes and observations on a few of the commoner objects of the Southern English Counties which have from time to time come under my notice, were originally written only for the purpose of amusing my dear old friend H. Stacy Marks, R.A., and the suggestion of their publication is owing to him. It is possible, as he said, that when published they may be found acceptable to some who, like himself, love nature for its own sake, untrammelled by the prepossessions that not unfrequently accompany that love among the votaries of science or sport.

The great fear that has suggested itself

to my mind is, that my readers may imagine
that I am attempting something after—however long after—Gilbert White. But though
I may indeed pray with the poet—

> Great prefect, in thy Heavenly Master's school,
> If there are places in the world to be
> For humble minds who own the same mild rule,
> Mine would I choose not all too far from thee—

yet nothing would be more distasteful to me,
or to the shade of him whose centenary we
have just celebrated, than such a comparison.
Mr. Marks used humorously to call these
letters my D.B. (Daines Barrington) letters:
but his tongue is privileged; for I can lay
claim to very little of the scientific knowledge
or to the patient method of investigation
which made White what he was; and my
excuse for accepting my friend's suggestion
reduces itself therefore to the somewhat lame
one, that there is always value in any records
of the ways of nature, no matter by whom

made, provided such records are written
truthfully, contemporaneously, and from
direct personal observation.

In justice to myself, I must add that these
are *bona fide* letters, written at the times
they are dated, and not in any sense com-
pilations ; and I must plead as my excuse for
the errors which will no doubt be detected in
those parts which relate to natural history,
my want of any complete collection of books
of reference on the subject.   As to the
illustrations, they are for the most part only
corrected reproductions of the little pen and
ink scribbles which I occasionally inserted in
my letters ; and in this form they will perhaps
harmonise better with the character of the
letters themselves than if they had been
more elaborated.   I have to acknowledge
my obligations to Mr. Marks for much help,
especially for the neat and careful way in
which he preserved the original letters ; and

to my nephew, Mr. C. R. L. Fletcher, Fellow of Magdalen College, Oxford, who has assisted me with the correction of the proof sheets.

RIVERSIDE, WALLINGFORD,
July 1893.

Fruit of the Eglantine.

CONTENTS

LETTER XXI

LETTER XXII

LETTER XXIII

LETTER XXIV

LETTER XXV

LETTER XXXIV

LETTER XXXV

LETTER XXXVI

LETTER XXXVII

ILLUSTRATIONS

FULL PAGE

IN THE TEXT

ERRATA

P. 55. *For* "worm in the bud" *read* "worm i' the but."
P. 82. *For* "Nutbornholm" *read* "Nunbornholme."

LETTER I

Country Life at Riverside—Painting out of doors—Picture of "The Garland"—Number of Flowers blooming at Michaelmas—Jam-making—Velvet Rose—Approach of Winter—Open-air Fête at Lockinge.

RIVERSIDE, WALLINGFORD,
4th October 1885.

DEAR MARCO—I am extremely sorry that you are unable to perform your promise of paying me a visit here. I am not in the least, as yet, tired of country life, and, were it not for the pleasure of seeing my old friends, have no wish to leave this place for a single day. I ought to be happy, for, in the possession of a nice house and pretty garden on the banks of Thames, the wish of my boyhood has been fulfilled. The moving waters across which I

B

see the sun rise almost every day lose none
of their charms on closer intimacy, and in my
garden I find delight and occupation for, I
am afraid to say, many beyond what are
usually called spare hours. This summer,
which was a dry and pleasant one, my painting has been mostly carried on out of doors.
I had a small tent put up on the lawn, in
which I arranged two models and a lay figure
with the accessories, from which I worked.
The picture represents three girls making garlands for some festivity, in the toned light of
a tent with a background of bright sunlight.
Poynter and Hodgson, the only two of my
artist friends who have seen the picture,
seemed very pleased with it, and, if I do not
spoil it in the finishing, I think it will do
fairly well. The fine weather has continued
into the autumn as yet, and in proof I may
mention that on Michaelmas day I counted
no less than seventy-one different flowers in
bloom, of course not all in perfection, but I
picked most assuredly seventy-one different

specimens and laid them out as a sort of flower-show on the table in my boat-house; notwithstanding its being the silly season, I refrained from troubling the papers on the subject.

Plums have been a wonderful crop, more like bunches of huge grapes than plums. Apples and walnuts too have done remarkably well, as have the vegetables, though peas and strawberries, owing to the dry weather, were rather a failure. Jam-making has been going on to a great extent. There is only the blackberry and damson yet to be made. Jam-making time used to be the delight of my childhood. My mother was a great hand at it, and now that we preserve our own fruit the old associations come back to me: the gently bubbling fruit and sugar in the polished preserving pans on the edge of the fire give off the same most delightful odour, and the mysteries of skimming, potting, tasting, and labelling are as attractive as ever to me.

My garden is stocked, in the matter of
flowers, with all the old-fashioned perennials

The Velvet Rose, from Gerard.

I can lay my hands on.   Amongst others, I
have a rose that is almost obsolete, at any rate

it is not to be found in the catalogues or
gardens of modern rose-growers.   It is called
the velvet rose, and boasts an ancestry quite
as old as the days of Queen Elizabeth ; it is
well and fully described by Gerard in his
Herbal, and no doubt must have been seen
and smelt by Shakespeare : possibly it was the
badge of the Lancastrians.   I prize it more
than any of the huge blooms of the hybrid
perpetuals, with their human names, which
figure in our rose shows ; it is small and
shows a tuft of orange gold stamens in its
centre, the contrast of which with the dark
velvety character of its petals is perfectly
Titianesque.

The yew hedges which I planted are fast
becoming clippable, the pleasure of doing
which I intend to reserve for myself.   The
autumn is now well upon us, as the colchicum
blooms bear witness.   The swallows are beginning to congregate on the river banks
previous to leaving.   Owls hoot and screech ;
when I go into the garden on starlight

nights I often hear them, as well as from up
above my head the curious cries of passing
birds, probably some sort of wild ducks.   I
no longer come across toads when gardening ;
they have no doubt betaken themselves to
their winter quarters amidst piles of swept-up
leaves or manure-heaps; in such places I have
discovered them in the winter or spring
snugly ensconced.

This summer a very successful and picturesque open-air fête was given by Lord and
Lady Wantage at Lockinge, about twelve
miles from here, to which we went.   The
guests were all dressed in the costume of the
time of Queen Elizabeth.   The weather was
very fine, and there were processions and
pageants got up with great taste and skill.
The grounds and park were well suited for
the purpose. The servants and peasants added
to the effect, for they also were in appropriate
dresses.   There was a quaint car with alle-
gorical figures in it, drawn by oxen with
gilt horns and adorned with garlands, which

would have greatly delighted you, dear Marco,
especially when, during one of the waiting
periods, these fine beasts lay down to rest.

G. D. L.

LETTER II

10th November 1885.

DEAR MARCO—The old house in which I
now live is built on the site of what was
formerly called "the middle wharf." There
are two wharves now existing here, the upper
and the lower wharves, which still do a considerable amount of business, chiefly in coal,
which is brought in barges from the Stafford-
shire coalfields by the canal which passes
through Coventry, Oxford, and Banbury.
The barge traffic formerly was also largely
employed in carrying barley and grain ; this
business has, however, for a long time ceased.
Of the middle wharf I found many traces
when the foundations of my new boat-house

were being excavated, a great quantity of coal being dug up from the edge of the river, as well as the remains of the old timbers of a canal-boat. The gentleman who purchased the property many years ago must in building have utilised some old house or other which no doubt was on the spot, for in effecting the considerable structural alterations which I made the builders came upon timber and brick walls of a much older character than the rest of the work. The house has been altered and enlarged by almost every one of its different owners at various times, and is in consequence very rambling and intricate in its internal arrangements, abounding in narrow back stairs, crooked passages, dummy windows, etc. The house was last used as a boarding-school for young ladies, and when I came to view it before buying it there were still a few little girls at work in the large class-room, to whom my intrusion must have been a source of curiosity and excitement. The lady who kept this

school added a number of bedrooms: there
were nineteen bed and dressing rooms altogether, but I am sorry to say only two of any
size. On various cupboard doors I found
many little pencil inscriptions, the work of the
school-girls, which may amuse you. They
are suggestive of the school life of former
days, with its likes and dislikes. "I love Ada
Lloyd," and beneath, "So do I." "I hate
Hetty Clarke and Emma Richings." "I
dislike Emma Richings, she tries to part
friends." "We are all going home next
Tuesday three weeks." "I hate ——" with
the name obliterated, and beneath, "The
person who wrote this is a ——" also obliterated. "I love Mary Davis and Ada
Lloyd." "We all do." And one, only one
male name, though this was cut in the wood,
"I love Edward." Who was Edward?

I found the garden in a very neglected
state. There was a cow feeding on the lawn,
and as the school washing was done at home,
a large part of the kitchen garden was used

for drying purposes. The windows were very rotten, so much so that I had to put in new ones in every case excepting two. Owing to some ill-advised internal alterations, the floors of the upper rooms in one part had fallen considerably, so that there were those sort of rolling hills and valleys in them that one comes across in old country hotels, and the external walls in parts were bulging out like the sides of an old-fashioned line-of-battle ship. I had some thoughts at one time of pulling the whole down and building a fresh house, but my architect very wisely deterred me, remarking "that any one can build a new house, but nobody an old one"; so, after a good deal of consideration and planning, the house was very effectually patched up, and, I am happy to say, without in the least losing its old-fashioned look and character.

There are some fine horse-chestnut trees at the back of the house, that is, if the river side is the proper front, a very fine walnut, and an interesting though not very handsome

sycamore in front : I call this latter tree interesting, for it is near the house and easily
seen from my bedroom window, and besides
having two starlings' nests in its bole it forms
a sort of rendezvous for all the birds in the

The part of the Sycamore Tree seen from my bed.

garden at all hours of the day. I have a good
binocular always at hand in my bedroom, by
means of which I obtain an insight into the
ways and doings of the birds on its branches ;
these observations can, in the early mornings
in summer, be carried on from my bed through

the open window, as the best part of the tree
is well seen from my pillow. Some friends
regard this tree as rather an eyesore, and
want me to cut it down, and for some reasons
I should not mind getting rid of it, mainly
perhaps on account of the aggravating way it
sheds its seed in every part of the garden;
but for the sake of the birds and the delightful shade, I feel I can put up with its other
disadvantages, so the tree is safe during my
time.

G. D. L.

LETTER III

1st February 1886.

DEAR MARCO—Perhaps, on the whole, I derive more amusement from the starlings than from any other birds. For one thing, they are so continually with us ; then they are so lively and cheerful in disposition—singing, chattering, and whistling at all seasons, even when the robins are silent. They are, of all birds that I know, most like human beings in their social and gregarious habits, for they seem to exist entirely in communities all the year round. The pluck with which they take their tub, when food is at its scarcest, washing themselves in the most complete and thorough manner at the edges of the river, even when

partly frozen, must command our admiration.
By the way, Marco, put pans of water in
your garden and ask your friends in St.
John's Wood to do likewise; the London
starlings and other birds will be very grate-
ful, and bathe in them continually.

Starlings are for ever doing something
or other, and whatever they do they do it
with a will. They have endless variety in
their conversation, and I am sure are fond of
play, dodging and jumping about one another
in the most ludicrous way. They are great
ventriloquists, as I have repeatedly noticed,
at times subduing their notes so as to sound
as if they came from a far distance; one I
often hear which imitates exactly the sound
of a man driving stakes as it would sound if
it were a long way off, and I have heard
one who crowed like a distant village cock.[1]

When a large flock of starlings is feeding

[1] I perhaps ought to state that this starling was in a cage that
hung on a cottage wall; but the bird had picked up the imitation
of its own accord, and rendered the effect of distance perfectly.

on the meadows, they cover a considerable patch of ground. The whole troop shifts along gradually against the wind; this shifting is done on the principle by which a boy takes a halfpenny from between two other halfpennies without touching it, the rearmost birds continually rising and flying over the heads of the others and settling in the front. Occasionally the whole flock rises and shifts in a mass. I have never been able to determine what it is they feed on : worms, no doubt, if they come across them, but the incessant picking-up motions must be occasioned by something far more numerous than worms. As you know, I never use a gun to help me in my observations of birds, and so have not examined their crops, but I have carefully searched the grass on our lawn after the starlings have been feeding on it, and beyond noticing the little holes made by the birds' beaks, have found nothing to indicate what the food might be. Most people must have remarked the way starlings feed along with

sheep and cattle, the hoofs of these no doubt
disturbing the ground and exposing their
prey to the birds, but what the particular
prey is I cannot tell; one thing is certain, it
must be very plentiful.   Starlings feed generally in company with rooks, though these

Flight of Starlings and Rooks.

latter no doubt seek larger objects, despising
such small fry as would content the starlings.
Anyhow, a flock of rooks and starlings must
make a very clean platter of their feeding-
ground before they leave it, searching as they
do every nook and cranny, and spread out in
such a broad phalanx.   When the rooks seek
new ground as they fly in extended fashion

high up, they are able to select a fresh place easily, and the starlings, knowing their sagacity in these matters, keep up with them, flying lower down and in a dense mass.

The starling is well built for his mode of life. He has a short, strong neck, rather long and pointed beak, powerful legs, and a short tail; his feathers are very glossy and water-proof, rather narrow and pointed in character, which helps the bird, when he gives a vigorous shake, to get rid of the raindrops easily. Starlings, like rooks, frequent the neighbour-hood of man, but never seem to get over the distrust with which they regard his actions; they will come for food in the winter if placed for them, but are exceedingly alert and watch-ful when thus feeding, in marked contrast to the robins, sparrows, or tomtits.

Blackbirds, thrushes, and robins have an entirely different way of feeding on the grass, and I imagine seek for a different sort of food. Instead of walking rapidly

about and continually pecking up something,
the solitary thrush takes a few hops and
remains dead still, his head raised slightly;
on perceiving his worm, or whatever it is,
he makes a sudden hop to the spot and
then proceeds to extricate it, giving it a
number of masticating pecks before swallow-
ing. Robins and blackbirds do the same,
all these birds being very silent, very swift
and observant, but doing everything with
a dead pause between. Not so the starling.
He bustles about pecking right and left
incessantly, which makes me think he feeds
not on worms, which wary creatures, having
such notice of the bird's proximity given
them, would easily escape by retiring into
their holes. Thrushes too are always alone
on the feed, whereas with starlings the more
the merrier. This flock-feeding saves a lot
of time spent in looking out for danger, as
the multitude of eyes in the skirmishing
party affords mutual safety to all, whereas
the solitary bird has to keep his eyes on

the look-out for his prey and his foes at
the same time.

This winter we have had a squirrel in
our garden. He chiefly frequents the walnut

Winter Aconites.

tree. He looks very pretty running over the
snow on the lawn in the morning sun. The
children place bread and walnuts for him,
which he condescends to take, and he has
become comparatively tame. The repeated
snow-storms and frosts have, I am sorry to

say, done much injury to some of the more
delicate of my plants, but the hardier ones
are all right. The spring flowers are very
backward; I have a few snowdrops, he-
paticas, and violets out. The winter aconites,

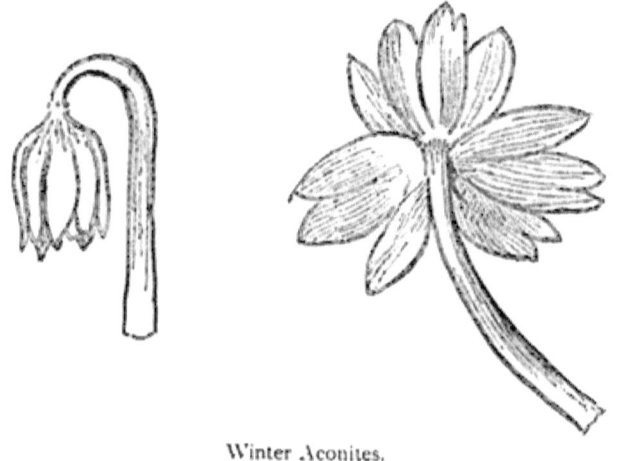

Winter Aconites.

the hardiest of all, do not seem to mind the
frost a bit, being frozen and drooping one
day, and reviving as if nothing had happened
immediately the weather is milder; they are
a most fascinating little flower, with quaint
green frills round their necks, and come up
into the light backwards, about which method

of procedure I must reserve what I have to say for another letter.

Trusting you and your picture are as well as can be expected, I remain, yours faithfully,

G. D. L.

LETTER IV

20th March 1886.

DEAR MARCO—Whilst we poor artists are
all struggling with our pictures, finishing and
getting them ready for the Exhibition, all the
little seeds and plants are bestirring themselves, much exercised as to the getting out
of their winter quarters beneath the ground,
and struggling to reach the upper air.
Warmth and light are the chief motive
powers in all cases, though there is considerable variety in the modes of operation.
Plants are divided by botanists into two
principal classes: Exogenous and Endogenous. Endogens, at least as far as we are

concerned in the garden, may be easily known and remembered as lilies and their kind ; with a few exceptions, all that are not lilies are Exogens. There is another class which comprises the mosses, lichens, etc., but they are more or less permanent plants, and do not have to struggle through the earth in the spring.

The exogenous and endogenous methods of pushing through the soil are exactly like the two ways a lady threads her needle : either with a screwed and pointed end as in the case of cotton, or with a loop as in the case of worsted. The exogen pushes through with a loop, whilst the endogen pierces through with a point.

The loop method is the most interesting to watch, and I will take that first. You know, I dare say, that plants, and indeed most livings things,[1] grow quickest in the dark ; warmth and darkness being very conducive to growth, as on the other hand cold

[1] As, for instance, babies.

and light act as retarding agents. The
frosts in winter expand and lighten the soil,
raising it up very much as yeast does the
dough ; this not only renders it soft and
easily pierced by the young plants, but also
allows the warmth of the sun to penetrate
more thoroughly. Under these conditions
the stalks begin to lengthen and push up-
wards, whilst the roots serve as anchors
below. At the end of exogenous stalks the
leaves and flowers grow in a bunchy way,
which, offering resistance to the earth, keeps
back the end of the stalks and forms the
loop. As the stalk keeps on pushing up
from below it gradually clears the bunch of
leaves from the soil ; it is then that the
retarding effect of light begins to tell, for
the upper side of the loop being more ex-
posed to its influence its growth is checked,
whilst the under or concave side, by going
on growing, straightens the stalk, and so the
young plant is gradually warped as it were
into shape. The little drawing of a syca-

more seed may help you to understand my
somewhat cumbrous description. Amongst
the lily tribes one often sees the flower
bending over and forming a loop; but the
flower will be found, in the first instance,
screwed up into a point, and does not curl

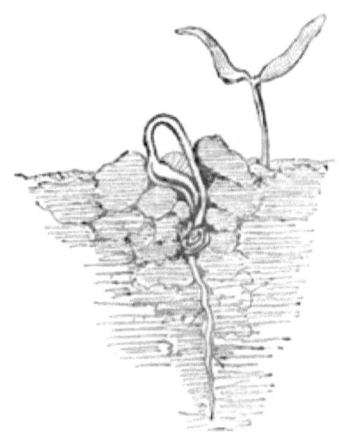

over until the stalk, which goes on growing
quickly in the dark pointed sheath of leaves,
pushes it through, when the weight of the
bloom tells and bends it over, as in the case
of the snowdrop or daffodil. But in both
the spike and the loop the retarding effect
of light and the accelerating power of dark-

ness, coupled with heat, are the main agents at work in forming and developing the growth.

The care with which Nature wraps up her treasures is very interesting. The soft woolly lining which so many seed-coverings have, and the papery filament which surrounds so many blooms when in embryo state, must afford great pleasure to any one who examines these things. The whity-brown paper which envelops the daffodil, especially noticeable in the poet's narcissus, always reminds me of the wrappings round the lower parts of the dolls in the toy-shop windows.

The long frosts have delayed the growth of all spring plants this year, so that my crocuses are only just fully out; but they seem all the finer for having been kept back, enjoying the lengthening sunlight which they get now. They are surrounded by innumerable bees all day long, some of which, through their eagerness to take advantage of

the first blossoms of the year, stay out too late and get overtaken by the night chill before they can reach their home.

The robins have still their winter tameness, and as I sow my annuals one will perch almost at arm's length, singing the sweetest little gentle song of congratulation.

Yesterday Alice and I rode over to Ewelme on our tricycles to get some watercresses. I thought of you much, especially when I saw the swans on the mill-pond at Benson. The little mill at Ewelme was burnt down last year and is now a most wonderfully picturesque ruin with the water tumbling over it in wild confusion.

I grieve to think of leaving here so soon, and that some of my greatest pets in the flower-garden will bloom and fade during the time I am hanging the pictures at the R.A.

G. D. L.

LETTER V

27th March 1886.

DEAR MARCO—I intended to have added something about crocuses to my last letter, but thought it long enough as it was. Perhaps you may have noticed that though the yellow and orange crocuses have far the largest bulbs, the blue, lilac, and white ones exceed them in the size of their flowers. Is it possible that this is due to the effect light has on them ? Photographers tell us, or did so years ago, that the sun's rays possess another power besides light and heat, which they call actinism ; it is this power which affects the salts of silver and turns them dark more than the light itself. This actinism is

found most in the blue and violet parts of
the spectrum and far less in the yellow and
orange; hence in the negative photograph
blue and violet objects, being most affected,
come out intensely dark, whereas reds,
yellows, and greens are rendered fainter;

Relative proportions of Yellow, Blue, and White Crocuses.

of course in the positive this is reversed,
the blue and violet parts being extra light,
whilst reds, greens, etc., print dark. Now
I cannot help thinking that this actinism
affects the blooms of plants, if it is not
indeed itself the retarding force in the ray

of light, and that thus the orange crocus, which absorbs most of the actinic ray, is somewhat retarded in its growth, at the same time that the white, blue, and violet blooms, which reflect these rays, attain a freer and larger, though a more slender growth. Of course this is only a theory of mine, and I intend looking out for examples amongst flowers with the different colours in the variety of their blooms. At present I can only think of two others besides the crocus, namely, yellow pansies, which generally run smaller than the deep violet, and the pinky-white blossoms of Alstrœmerias, which are with me always larger than the tawny or orange-coloured ones.

A very ghastly fate sometimes overtakes the crocus. On a bright sunny day, when the blooms are all spread open like stars, it occasionally happens that a snow-shower comes on suddenly in the afternoon before the poor things can close up, and numbers receive a plug of snow into their hearts, which, as night

comes on, freezes into solid ice. I can
imagine nothing worse.

It is always the late snows and frosts that
do the most damage.

All growing vegetation has the power of
absorbing and storing heat ; this heat we find
stored up in wood, which when burnt gives
it out again. My brother, Sir Bradford,
tells me that in India all growing leaves
feel cool to the touch, no doubt because
they absorb and retain the heat rays, but
that dead leaves, having not this property,
feel intensely hot, radiating the heat as a
piece of stone or iron would.

G. D. L.

LETTER VI

14th May 1886.

I WAS reminded of you, dear Marco, this
morning, by the vast quantities of birds that
were busy on the lawn in front of my bedroom window; after the heavy rains of the
last two days they were all at it, picking
away to feed their rising families: starlings,
thrushes, blackbirds, sparrows, robins, and
wagtails. The air swarmed with swallows,
and when my wife opened the window down
came a perfect shower of martins which had
been perched on the eaves above. I never
saw a scene of greater activity, the wonder
being that there were no collisions in the air

D

between the slower-flying birds and the
swallows. The wagtails were very busy,
both the gray and the pied ones : these latter
extremely genteel and dapper, "in evening
dress," as my niece Katie once said.

The swallows have returned to their
nests in the boat-house, and it is delightful

Bird's-eye view of a Swallow.

to look down at them from the balcony as
they fly in through the arch beneath you.
This bird's-eye view of a swallow as he
enters the arch is quite beautiful : his tail
expanded shows the little crescent-shaped
string of white spots on it, and altogether
the bird looks like an exquisite tropical

butterfly. I say as he enters the arch, for when he shoots out again his tail is closed and the speed and suddenness of the exit almost defies observation. This tropical beauty is not surprising, as I believe swallows are related to the sun-birds and humming-birds, and the wonder to me is that they should ever leave the warmer and sunnier latitudes to return to the dark holes and corners where they build their nests, with such a fitful climate as we enjoy in England.

The river is in high flood, and should it rise much more the swallows will be unable to reach their nests, as the entrance archway will be closed up. Yesterday the weather was wild, with a driving rain and northerly wind all day long ; but it was, in an ornitho-logical way, most interesting, as we were visited by a large flock of what I believe were terns, possibly they were black-headed gulls, but I am nearly sure they were terns. My only book on birds is Bewick, and his account of either bird is very meagre ; but in the

Dictionary of the Thames (which contains a
capital article on the birds) I found that terns
have frequently been seen about here, and
one, "the sooty tern," was shot here in 1869.
I did not shoot any, and all I can send you
is my account of how they looked and what
they did ; no doubt you will be able to tell
me whether they were terns or not.

At first sight I took them for a flock of
pigeons, but their rapid flight and the way
they hawked up and down over the water
soon convinced me they were sea-birds of
some sort.   I placed myself at the boat-house
window so as to get as good an observation
as possible.   I counted nine of them, and as
they flew past repeatedly very close to me,
I noticed that they varied a good deal in their
plumage ; one especially was distinctly smaller
and darker, the head and body brownish
black, the belly and wings of a dusky gray ;
the others varied in colour, some appearing
lighter than others, and the black on the
heads varied also ; their general colour was a

THE BOAT-HOUSE, RIVERSIDE.

To face page 36.

beautiful ash-gray, white underneath, and
black caps on their heads. They flew up
and down the river, over a space of nearly
half a mile, going almost out of sight and
returning again continually. They were on
the sharp look-out for fish, hawking much
over the shallow flooded places. Every now
and again one would execute a sort of somer-
sault in the air, and shoot down with amazing
speed, striking the water with a dash and a
splash ; when they did this near me, I could
see that they often carried off a fish, though
not always, which they must have gorged on
the wing as they never stopped for a moment,
but dashed along with their companions. It
was a most delightful sight, and I longed for
you. I remember having once before seen
a solitary one of these birds, hawking up and
down over the same places ; it was in the
afternoon of a very rainy day with high wind,
but I forget the time of the year.

My flowers are rejoicing in the rain, but I
have to keep a sharp look-out for snails and

slugs; it does not do to trust entirely to the
birds. I found a favourite clump of St. Bruno's
lilies had been attacked by the small flat snail,

Parrot Tulips.

of which there are great quantities this year.
With soot and vigilance I think I have saved
my anthericum. My tulips have been simply
perfect; I made some studies in oil from them,

only the worst of flower-painting is that no pigment comes the least like nature, whilst the flowers keep moving and altering every instant as you paint. Do you know the parrot tulips? in colour and quaint form these surpass all; some I have of exquisite feathery grace, quite Venetian in colour, with dusky gray and golden streaks on red grounds of various shades, from bright orange to deep scarlet lake.

Gerard says of the tulip that it is named after the "Dalmatiane or Turke's cap, called Tulipan, Tolepan, Turban, and Turfan," and that it is a flower "with which all studious and painefull Herbarists desire to be better acquainted with, because of that excellent diversitie of most brave flowers which it beareth."

G. D. L.

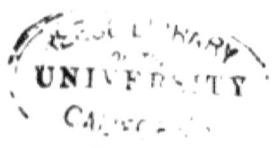

LETTER VII

16*th May* 1886.

DEAR MARCO—Many thanks for your interesting and prompt reply to my last letter.
I have now no doubt about the birds in
question being terns. Your description
tallies exactly with what I saw, and though
I did not notice their tails, I remember that
the general aspect of their wings and tails
was that they were long and pointed. The
smaller and darker bird may have been a
sooty tern, which I believe is scarce in
England. I see by the papers the floods
have been very high in the Severn valley
(the highest since 1837), and it is quite
possible, as the winds have been west and

north-west and very strong, that these birds
have come from the estuary of the Severn,
over the Cotswolds, to our river, and worked
their way down to us. They flew along
together backwards and forwards, exactly as
you describe, "like spaniels hunting a field."
They also uttered a shrill cry every now and
then, and occasionally seemed to hover like
the kestrel. My brother Robert had a
black-headed gull, and I remember that the
black on its head completely covered it,
whereas these birds had only a sort of black
cap.

I am sorry you are not *very* fond of tulips
and peonies, as I like both so greatly. If
the weather permits, I will send Agnes some
of my tulips; perhaps you will like them
better in the cut state than when seen as
planted in the abominable cockney fashion in
masses. The Gesner, the parrot, and the
cottager's tulips are much the most beautiful
of any, except perhaps *Tulipa Greigii*, or
Turkestan tulip, which is very early and of

an intensely bright orange scarlet with
curiously spotted foliage.

A robin has built his nest in an old garden

Pump in which the Robin built.

pump, thus preventing our using it; I suppose
the young ones will issue from the spout.

It is sad to have to confess that we have
no nightingales at Wallingford.   I have been

told they built here formerly, but that for
many years they have deserted the place.
There are plenty of shrubberies and coppices
about of the sort that the bird delights in, and
I was at a loss to account for the absence of
the famous songster. I am now convinced,
however, that it is owing to the increase of
the rookeries here and in the immediate
neighbourhood. There are two rookeries in
Wallingford : one in the castle grounds and
another in Mr. Hayllar's garden, which is
next to my own. On the Oxfordshire side of
the river there are three more large rookeries:
at Howbery, Crowmarsh, and Mongewell.
It is not the rookeries themselves that drive
away the nightingales, but the shooting of
the young rooks which goes on during the
month of May. The constant banging away
that takes place at this time, when the nightingales are busy on their nests, would no doubt
be quite sufficient to scare them from the
place. I have to walk to Shillingford, about
two miles, to hear the exquisite songsters.

There by the bridge they abound, as well as
in the Wittenham woods a little higher up
the river; there are no rookeries near these
places and consequently no spring shooting.
This rook shooting is defended by the lovers
of the sport as a necessary act, and one that
is beneficial to the rooks, as they say if the
young rooks were not thus thinned out the
rookery would in time be abandoned altogether; they say also that young rooks make
a very good pie; I have never tasted one, so
I cannot give any opinion as to this, but I
must say this rook shooting seems to me
about the most cruel and barbarous of all the
various processes of animal destruction which
pass by the name of sport.   The time chosen
for the slaughter is just before the young
birds are able to fly, when they sit perched
about on the branches around the nests.   The
shooting is of a difficult character, as the gun
has to be held rather perpendicularly.   The
moment it begins the old birds fly off, though
anxiety for their young ones keeps them near

the scene of destruction. They generally fly round and round, just out of range, above the nests, uttering the most unmistakable cries of misery as they see one after another of their offspring fall fluttering to the ground through the branches of the elms. It is this protracted torture to the parent birds which imparts to the sport its special feature of cruelty; the fact that many of the young birds lodge wounded amongst the branches in lingering pain adds as well to the gruesomeness of this kind of slaughter. The demoralising effect on the crowd of bumpkin urchins who look on should also be taken into account.

Yesterday I found a thrush's nest, which I had been watching for some time, abandoned, with three half-fledged young in it, evidently killed by the cold rain, and my neighbour's son rescued a young rook that was flapping in the river.

I heard to-day, for the first time this year, the sedge-warbler in the shrubbery keeping

up that incessant "cheep-cheep, chissock-
cheep," etc., that caused us to christen him
"the scissors bird."

This evening I also heard the landrail or
corncrake. It frequents the meadow opposite
us, and all the time the hay crop is growing
we hear the grating cries of this bird, especially at night.

I should be quite happy here if only I
could see a little more of my old friends.   I
enjoy, however, greatly writing to you, and
am very glad you like to hear from me.
Many thanks for drinking my health.

G. D. L.

LETTER VIII

1st June 1886.

DEAR MARCO—"A dripping June brings all in tune," though whether my neighbour who began cutting his hay yesterday thinks so is open to doubt. The birds seem to like the rain, at least they sing incessantly when it rains, especially thrushes and blackbirds. I am no great admirer of the blackbird; there is too much reiteration in his song, and he has such self-assertive and aggressive manners. When disturbed by a cat or anything, he gives off a loud and incessant "cheek-cheek-cheek," which serves to spread the alarm all round. His boldness is amazing; when beneath the strawberry

netting, unless you raise it and make a dash,
he will refuse to budge, merely hopping along
farther away. When he alights on a branch
or on the lawn, he raises his expanded tail up
and down in the most conceited fashion, and
indeed, were it not for his handsome figure
and something Shakespeare said of his orange
tawny bill, I should positively hate him.

The people here have a curious superstition about the wandering German bands that
visit us at times. It is that they invariably
bring rain. When they see them crossing
the bridge they say, "There come the
Germans, it will rain to-morrow." My
gardener firmly believes in this. I suppose
it is the old spirit of barbarism that lingers
in the country, which in old times used to
burn witches and shrew mice.

I am amused with watching the ways of
worms. If you turn over a heap of rotten
leaves, the large fat worms that are discovered remain quite still, trusting thus to
escape observation, but if you take a stone

and press the earth down with it anywhere
you will be almost certain to see a wonderfully bright and clean worm issue forth a little
distance off, endeavouring with the utmost
speed to make his escape.

The worms now are all extremely busy
collecting little heaps of the wych-elm blossoms, which fall in quantities all over the
paths and lawn.   This fresh green food must
be very acceptable to them after their long
fast, and you see little piles of it collected
by the worms in every direction.

On warm nights in September I have
seen, in the shrubbery paths of my neighbour's garden, luminous worms crawling
rather quickly in little serpentine lines on the
ground.   They are quite bright, with a phos-
phorescent glow, about two inches or a little
less in length, and luminous throughout their
whole body.   When I examined one I found
it to be a sort of " hundred legs " or myriapod,
much like those sometimes found inside apricots.   It was exceedingly fragile; in picking

E

it up I only secured the head and part of
the body; this remained luminous in my hand,
and when smashed and rubbed on my finger
the finger became luminous. It had a small
yellowish-brown head with slender antennae,
as the myriapods usually have. There are
a great many pear and apple trees in the
shrubbery where I saw these creatures.

Two sparrows have been most persistent
in building their nest behind the wheel and
chain that raises the portcullis of my boat-
house; I have done all I could to frighten
them away, but in vain. I found out where
the nest was, though I could not see or get at
it, so I stuffed the aperture up with paper
and watched through the crack of the door
to see what would happen. After a bit the
cock appeared; at first sight of the obstruction he flew away, but afterwards grew bold,
and tried in every way to effect an entry.
I saw he had something in his beak, a small
grub it was, and as I then felt sure the young
must be already hatched I removed the

obstruction, since which the old birds go in and out in peace. Sparrows are almost considered as vermin by most people, but when they have their young to feed they must consume an immense quantity of insects and grubs. I am very glad that Agnes liked the tulips, and that you too acknowledged their beauty.

G. D. L.

LETTER IX

22nd June 1886.

DEAR MARCO—You ask me to discuss the bullfinch question. I have more than once had a bullfinch in a cage, and delight much in the quaint forms, the exquisite colouring, and the queer tricks and fancies of the birds ; but of their wild state I confess to knowing very little. In captivity they seem capable of great affection, and like many other birds have distinct preferences for certain people. One of mine would only bob and bow, put his tail on one side, and utter his little song to people with black or very dark eyes ; he knew me perfectly well, but would never

favour me with his tricks, so that whenever
I wanted to show him off I had to send for
my housekeeper's little girl Rhoda, in whose
dark eyes the bullfinch delighted. We have
visits from these birds occasionally in autumn
and winter, and it is easy to recognise their
rather melancholy pipe or toot, but they
never build with us.

When I had a cottage at Henley I saw
them at all times in the little garden; no
doubt they came across from the thick plant-
ations of Park Place. Holly-berries appeared
to be much esteemed by them. My friend
Miss Stapleton, who lived next door, encouraged them, and I do not think her garden
suffered in consequence, as she always had
very abundant crops of everything. Our
friend Wells, who lives at Holmbury in
Surrey, complains bitterly of the devastations
of the bullfinch, and he has them shot; he
told me he found their crops filled with buds.
His place, as you know, is surrounded by
woods and thick cover, and no doubt the

birds abound.   Frank Walton, who lives
close to Wells, also complains of their depre-
dations.   I am afraid the fact of their eating

Fruit of the *Rosa rugosa.*

buds cannot be denied ; but for my own part
I should prefer the society of this beautiful
little living combination of black, gray, and
rose-colour to the preservation of a few
hundred extra buds in my garden.

Possibly after all, too, the partial destruction of buds is more or less good for the trees; there is a distinct tendency in highly cultivated trees and plants to send out rather more buds than are wanted, so that disbudding is often resorted to by the gardener.

Roses are of the same family as the apple, as my sketch of the *Rosa rugosa* shows, and have generally a great superabundance of buds, so that even the little "worm in the bud" sometimes does good in the thinning process; also the caterpillar, by thinning the leaves and allowing the sun to get at the fruit, when his work is not in excess, does less harm than many people imagine; no one can suppose that the vast quantities of worm-eaten apples that fall could ever have ripened successfully.

There is a convenient fact in favour of most insects and animals of prey, which is that they seem almost invariably to choose their food from the weakest and sickliest parts of vegetation; strong and vigorous growth is very seldom attacked; when some-thing ails the plant the aphis is sure to be attracted to it. In the same way snails and slugs greatly prefer those parts of a plant that are in semi-decay, thus acting in their legitimate capacity of scavengers, though no doubt at times they will eat healthy growing things, especially in dry weather, just as birds eat fruit in the hot weather when their ordinary food is scarce; but as a general rule the slug and snail live chiefly on decaying vegetation.

The fact is, the general balance of power is well kept if Nature is not interfered with; but if once you begin shooting bullfinches, you scare away the robins and tits, thereby allowing the lacquey and ermine moth an undue advantage.

I confess I do not like to hear of a brother artist who prefers a pint or two more of gooseberries or plums in his inside, or the threepence the fruit would produce in his pocket, to the sweet companionship of the

birds in his gardens. Even if the bird is a
thief, have we no fellow-thievish feeling for
him? You, dear Marco, I know, will never
countenance the destruction of birds in any
way, and I am sorry that any of our brethren
should join the ranks of the bumpkin gar-
deners in their ignorant crusade.

Fly-catchers build their nests in my
garden every summer. They are very dar-
ing in the choice of the place: one pair had a
nest between a climbing rose and the wall of
the boat-house, not a yard from a pump which
is continually used for watering purposes, and
another in a hole in a wall a few feet from
the ground. They also build in the sycamore tree. They are particularly partial to
perching on the posts of the tennis-nets, or
on the wirework which surrounds the court,
and will even do this when a game is going
on, every now and then executing their little
hovering flight after flies and returning to
their post. On a summer morning I can see
them from my bed catching flies beneath the

sycamore, dropping as it were from the branches into the air and returning to them in the prettiest way imaginable.

It would have gladdened your heart to have witnessed what I did last Sunday: a whole brood of young tomtits (eight or nine at the very least), on their first day's flight, perched about among my rose bushes in the morning sun ; they were so delightfully tame as to allow us to approach quite close ; they pruned their little new wings, gave out their little song one to another, and seemed so perfectly happy hopping and flitting about, it was most fascinating. At length, at some signal from the old birds, I suppose, the whole took flight, reaching the sycamore tree in safety, I am happy to say.

G. D. L.

LETTER X

15th July 1886.

DEAR MARCO—Our big chub have returned to their haunt by the side of the
boat-house. I count about seven of them,
mostly eighteen inches long. They seem
to know quite well the time we have our
tea in the little room in the boat-house;
as we usually feed them with bread, they
have become very tame and bold. It
affords us much amusement to watch them
feed; the pieces of bread have to be too
large for any of the swarm of smaller fish,
amongst which the large chub dash in and
carry off their prize with a swirl and flourish

of their tails.   These big chub vary in colour
a good deal, but all have large white mouths
and dark tails.   They seem to exercise
caution, and never take the bread at once,
rising and looking at it two or three times
first before they make up their minds.

When the long ribbon-like water-grass
is fully grown, if on a sunny day you look
down into it you will presently become aware
of a large shoal of roach feeding ; they do
not show at first very distinctly, but in the
twist they give when breaking off pieces of
the weed, their beautiful orange fins and
silvery sides attract immediate attention.
They feed or browse very like a herd of
cows.   At times one may be seen floating
head downwards, and all are very tranquil
in their enjoyment of the sun.   When alarmed
they seem to vanish rather than dart away,
hiding, I suppose, in the thick of the weeds ;
in a few moments they will appear again a
short distance off.   Predatory fish like perch
or pike do not congregate, but are gener-

ally solitary in their habits, whilst the other
sorts seem to know the safety of numbers,
and feed in shoals like sheep, or rooks, or
starlings.   A young jack is always seen
quite by itself, lying very still ; but perch
keep up a certain amount of companionship
with one another.   Perch hunt and capture
their prey very much as cats do, getting
round corners and amongst posts and weeds,
from whence they dart out with a sudden
rush of three or four yards ; these rushes
are easily seen, the small fish jumping clean
out of the water in every direction, the back
fin of the perch itself being sometimes seen
above water.   I do not know how jack take
their prey, but they lie like logs at the
bottom amongst the weeds, their eyes being
placed so that they can see well all above
them ; their mouths are so large and well
set with teeth that there is little chance of
escape for anything once seized.   A fisherman told me they seize their prey cross-
wise, and do not swallow it at once, but hold

it in their mouths, as a cat will a bird or
mouse, for some time, gorging it afterwards
slowly.

I wish I knew a little more about spiders;
I am sorry to say I am very ignorant on the
subject.   Of course I have read the gossipy
books about the gossamers, the trap-door,
the water, and the jumping spiders, and
their spinnerets and so on; but the
information in these books which my boys
have given them always stops short of what
I want to know: for instance, what are
those round-bodied spiders with very long
hair-like legs?   Harvestmen, I think I have
heard them called; perhaps they are not
spiders at all; at any rate they are inexplic-
able to me: what they live on, how they
catch it, whatever it is, where they go to in
the winter, etc.   I have only found them
myself in summer time; behind old boards,
on old walls and rubbish heaps, any amount
of them of all sizes can be found.   They run
with speed on being alarmed, and seem not

in the least to mind the loss of a leg or two. I have found them with their bodies sunk in holes and their legs extended over the edges; when disturbed they raise themselves like a gun in a barbette battery and make off in a great hurry ; is this their usual strategy for capturing their prey ? or what ?   Then there is another sort of spider with a bright green body, rather round in shape, which comes tumbling out of the rose-buds or leaves when you go to pick a rose ; it is usually on rose bushes, but I cannot see that it feeds on the aphidae, as it is often on bushes where no flies are found ; the books I have read say nothing of this fellow.   I found out that earwigs can walk on spiders' webs; I watched one do so ; it went about quite deliberately, and seemed to eat or suck sundry small midges which were in the web: the web was outside my window, and the spider was in his corner with as much as he wanted.

One never knows what millions of spiders'

webs there are in a garden until after a very heavy dew or white frost in autumn; then every possible corner and twig is seen to be covered with them. On my yew hedge they are innumerable. No doubt the cobwebs get collected on the wings of the little wrens and tits that frequent these hedges, and serve to glue the materials together with which their little compact nests are made. These webs too serve as so many delicate elastic stays to the young shoots of yew, and by their numbers must protect them much from the rough winds; when you see the young shoots bending over to one another you will find they are united by webs. But how, when you think of the millions of webs in every direction, flies, midges, or gnats escape at all is very wonderful; a yew hedge is always crowded with these flies when wet weather sets in, and if you beat the hedge swarms of midges, etc., will fly out as if no such things as spiders' webs existed there.

This June my garden has been very
beautiful, roses and other flowers doing very
well ; our strawberries were not, however, so
plentiful as usual.

G. D. L.

LETTER XI

18th September 1886.

DEAR MARCO—The summer this year has
been remarkably fine, not perhaps as dry as
'85, but as what rain we had mostly fell in
the night (at least in this neighbourhood), the
fine days were many and very delightful.
The river was very free of weeds, which I
suppose was owing partly to the severe protracted frosts of winter, and partly to the
spring floods, which were unusually strong.
During the last two or three days I have
noticed quantities of floating lumps of minute
vegetation, which when examined are found
to have soft mud and sand attached to the
roots, and are rendered buoyant by numbers

of gas bubbles evolved from the growth.
This small water-moss, or whatever it is, as
the gas bubbles accumulate, gets buoyed up
from the bottom of the river, carrying with it
some of the soil attached to the rootlets ; in
ponds one often sees this stuff, which at last
accumulates on the surface in a disagreeable
way, but on the river it floats down and trans-
plants itself with its little mass of travelling
soil. I have very little doubt it rises thus to
the top, as some larger water - weeds do,
during its blooming period, and sinks again
to the bottom for the winter. If you squeeze
one of these lumps, so as to set the bubbles
at liberty, it will sink directly.

September is just the month for spiders,
and I get much amusement from watching
them. In the boat-house there is a grated
window which does not open, and, being out
of the way, is entirely given up to the spiders ;
every corner of it and of the embrasure has
numberless cobwebs, whilst across and across
in every direction the wheel webs are spun

at every conceivable angle; and yet I watched
a gnat for a long time sailing slowly amongst
the webs with apparently no inconvenience;
how he managed it I cannot tell, unless his
shrill humming was his safeguard, warning
him by his possibly acute sense of sound of
the proximity of things, or it may be the touch
of his delicate feet was so soft that adhesion
did not take place. I am convinced he did
once or twice touch the webs, as the spiders
now and then gave little jerks to the lines of
the webs which ran to their corners. All at
once the gnat began one of those dancing
movements which gnats do sometimes, and
are so rapid as almost to render them invisible,
and immediately was caught by his wings in
a web. The gnat at once resorted to the well-
known device of simulating death, remaining
perfectly motionless; this saved his life, at
least as long as I remained, for the spider,
after a jerk or two, took no further notice.

The swallows are preparing to leave us;
the six nests inside the boat house and the

one in the piazza above are all deserted,
though three or four young birds still roost
on some iron staple-rings which are used to
tie the boats to. I took two, thus roosting,
up carefully in my hands and carried them

Young Swallows on the look-out for food in the nest in the Piazza.

out to show my children ; afterwards I placed
them back on the ring, when I was much
pleased and astonished to find they relapsed to
sleep again as though nothing had happened.

You might mention a great many wild
animals before you would guess the one that

was caught in my garden two days ago. No
other than a reindeer. The fact was, Wallingford was visited by a travelling circus last
week, and this beast had broken his chain,
swam a good part of the river, and landed
on my garden. Here he browsed away finely,
judging from the tracks of his curious hoofs.
The men from the circus had no difficulty in
securing him, as he had part of his chain on,
and was quite tame. I gave some of the
manure he left to some Iceland poppies I
have growing, as I thought it appropriate,
and might amuse them.

The circus was a very good one, and had
a negro lion-tamer, a performing bull, two
elephants (mother and calf), and two clowns,
one of whom informed us that he had a hero
for his father and a " Shero" for his mother.
It was very interesting to see the elephants
led down to the river for a bath and drink ;
they made huge holes in the gravelly bottom,
and seemed to enjoy the water very much.

                                        G. D. L.

LETTER XII

17th October 1886.

DEAR MARCO—I take great interest just
at this time in the seediness of my garden ;
seeds and seed-cases are perhaps the most
wonderful of any of the parts of plant life.
The theories of germs, fertilisation, and the
origin and perpetuation of species have been
so thrashed out by the scientists lately that,
even if I were able, I have no wish to discuss
the subject in a letter to you ; but there is
much pleasure to be derived by any ordinary
observer who has a garden in the study of the
various forms of seeds and of the construction
of their cases.   Has it ever struck you, as an
artist, that there is more picturesque architec-

tural structure displayed in the seed and its
case than in all the rest of the plant and its
parts? Flowers are very beautiful, but the
coloured petals of which they are usually
formed possess not half the architectural
beauty of the seed-receptacle. Take for instance a poppy-head of seed, with its cup and
ornamental little roof-top, beneath the eaves
of which are the little windows through which
the seeds fall out when ripe ; the flower when
in bloom is but a tumbled mass of loveli-
ness compared to this compact and neat
arrangement, which may be considered as a
regular little house with thousands of little
lives within it. Look at the wonderful combination of strength and lightness displayed
in the walnut shell, the picturesqueness of the
covering of the horse-chestnut, or the quaint-
ness of the winged seeds of the sycamore :
how different they all are, and how artistic.

The seed-heads of the lily tribes, again,
are extremely full of artistic interest. Most
of the spring flowering sorts have drooping

or bent over flowers, which arrangement

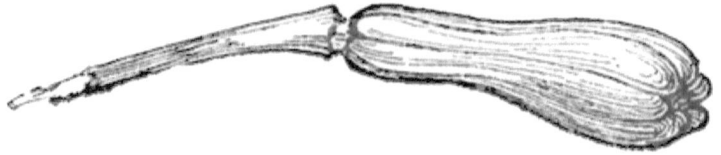

Seed-pod of Orange Lily.

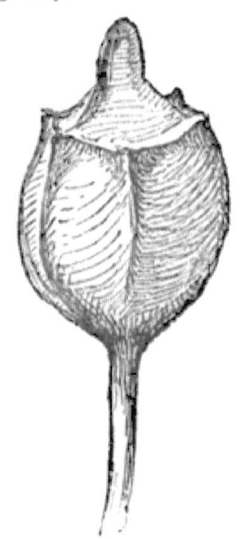

Seed-pod of Alstrœmeria.

Seed-pod of *Iris sibirica*.   Section of pod of *Iris sibirica*.

serves to protect the pollen from spring winds

and rain. The crown imperial and fritil-
laries in general, the snowdrops, the daffodil,
and most of the early blooming lilies are
examples of this ; but as the seed-heads ripen
they straighten themselves up, and in this
position get more warmth and light. All
these seed-heads have great character, reminding one of the beauties of Gothic archi-
tecture, and resembling knights' maces, or
beautiful vases or chalices with quaint lids to
them. The crown imperial seed-case, which
is the exact counterpart of a mace, will
straighten out and up until it surmounts the
tuft of green leaves that crests the bloom,
which would otherwise shade and render its
ripening difficult. The packing of the seeds
within these cases is equally beautiful in
arrangement, and differs greatly according to
the character and shape of the seed.

The seed-cases of the larger division of
plants which are not lilies are likewise infin-
itely various, and many of great beauty and
picturesqueness. The violet, for instance,

has a large and beautiful pod possessing the
scent and somewhat of the colour of the flower;

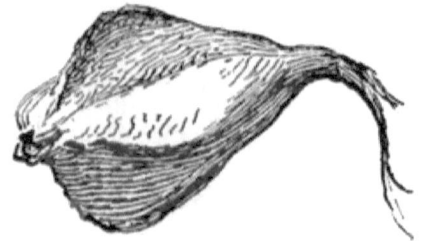

Biretta-like seed-pod of *Œnothera taraxifolia*.

when the seed is ripe the pod splits open
down its six seams, and forms quite a pretty

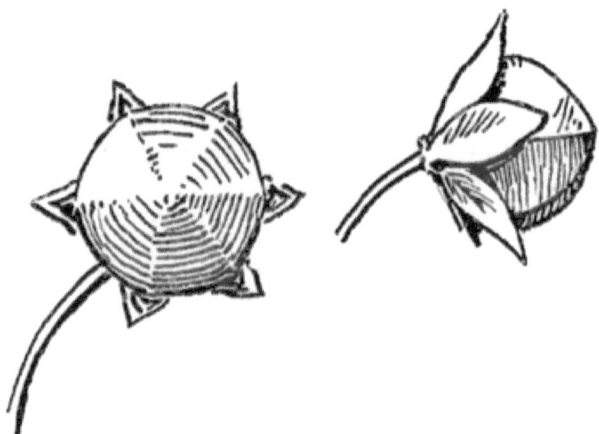

Seed-pod of Violet.

flower, so to speak, for the second time.
The seeds themselves are intensely slippery,

which allows them to fall readily about and
down into the chinks and holes in the earth.

Seed-cases of Snapdragons.

Again, how grotesquely comic are the Snap-

dragon seed-pods, at the same time how fine
and grand in line; they are like the skulls of

some animal, with eye-holes and nasal bones,
also a little like in profile to a prawn's head.
When empty, these dry heads form the most
tempting harbours of refuge to small insects,

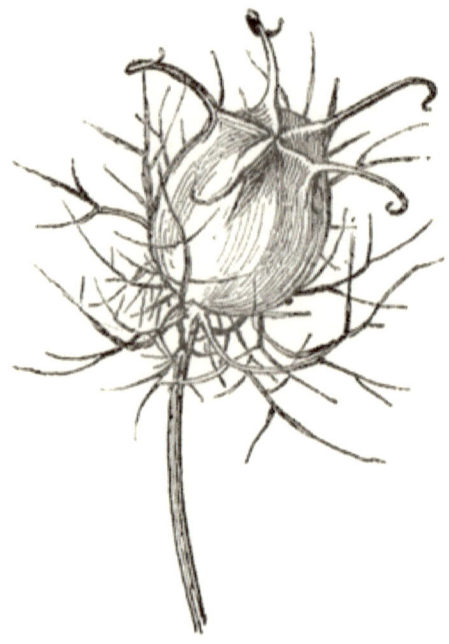

Seed-case of *Nigella Damascena.*

one or two of which crawled forth from the
specimen I have drawn for you. Nigella, or
"love in a mist," has a seed-pod reminding
us of Albert Durer's art, weird and grotesque
in the highest degree.

Many plants depend on the edible character of the coverings of the seeds for the dissemination of the seed itself; the rose family
do so almost entirely, birds and man stepping
in to assist as it were.   Hips and haws, plums,
apples and pears, currants, gooseberries, and
elders, are often sown by birds.   I am continually finding the three last growing in odd
places, sown by the birds.

The largest flower does not by any means
always have the largest seed.   Butcher's-
broom, which is a curious evergreen of the
lily tribe, and nearly related to asparagus,
has a flower no bigger than a pin's head right
in the centre of the green leaf, yet the seed,
a solitary one, is as large as a pea, and contained in a crimson berry still larger.   Then
there is the fig.   The bloom of this I can never
discover at all; the little green figs seem to
appear with the buds at the close of winter,
and go on swelling up until they ripen, full of
hundreds of seeds.   I am very partial to
green figs, and have a tree in a cool green-

house, in which it ripens two crops of figs a year, with only the sun to warm it. The subject of seeds is endless, my dear Marco, and the various methods Nature employs in dissemination would demand a volume for themselves ; it is a dry topic, however, and I will not bore you with it more at present.

Four or five swallows still fly round our sycamore, and still roost in the boat-house of nights ; thrushes and blackbirds have commenced to sing again at intervals ; the owls at night are very noisy, squeaking and "too-whooing" in quite a comic way at times. I picked up an owl's feather the other day, which I send you ; you will easily see by its extremely soft, downy character that it is an owl's, and it accounts in some way for the perfect silence of the flight of the bird.

G. D. L.

LETTER XIII

1st November 1886.

DEAR MARCO—I am not likely to forget
you down here, as the birds continually
remind me of you; whenever I see any of
them doing something odd or interesting,
I long for your presence. The other day I
witnessed what was to me quite a novelty
in the actions of the kingfisher; this bird, as
you no doubt know, generally sits on some
coign of vantage overhanging the edge of the
stream, darting at its prey head first, and
making off with it in its mouth when successful. The one I saw acted differently; the
river was swollen with rain, and the bird

flew out from the bank a short distance into
the air, performed a sort of hovering motion
over the water in little circles for a few
seconds, and then struck down on to the
surface with so much speed and violence,

Kingfisher hovering.

that I could hear the splash from our dining-
room window, quite fifty yards off. It reminded me of the actions of the terns I wrote
to you about in a former letter. The bird
seemed unsuccessful in his first attempt, and
in a short time he repeated the movement;
this time he made off altogether, as the birds

G

do generally when they have caught their fish,
so I concluded he had captured something.

The hovering action was peculiar, as it
was not like that of the hawk with the head
and body level, but with the head slightly
raised, as I have endeavoured to sketch it for
you ; the difficulty with me is how he could
watch the object he intended to strike with
his head thus raised. If you meet any of
your ornithological friends, perhaps you will
kindly inquire as to these curious movements
of the bird. I am not disposed to enter into
the discussion of the destructiveness of birds
in gardens with your correspondent. I think
Mr. Morris of Nutbornholm Rectory has
summed up the matter very conclusively in
his little pamphlet on bird murder ; I will
send it to you, and you can give it to your
friend. I have read it with great interest ;
the arguments seem to me to be well stated,
and the evidence, strong and conclusive.

The heavy rain last night has brought
down vast quantities of leaves, the flower-

beds and lawns being covered with them and débris of all sorts. At this time I am busy cutting down, cleaning up, dividing, and transplanting, and am much amused by the general sort of feasting that is going on amongst the birds, worms, snails, etc., all anxious to lay up as much nutriment as possible before the approach of winter. The worms are having a grand time gathering over their holes heaps of leaves which are gradually drawn below with a sort of funnel-shaped twist. The light-coloured end of the worm, which is its tail, is capable of being flattened out very broad, and affords the creature a fulcrum to work from, as it keeps it below in its hole, stretching out to its work with the rest of its body.

Then there are the innumerable host of small flat snails : little scraps of things, some black, some gray, and some yellowish in colour. The common tabby snail has already begun to hibernate. I found five or six stowed away, a day or two ago, behind a heap of flower-pots. I do not know whether

these smaller snails hibernate, at anyrate
they do not do it for nearly so long a period
as the larger ones, and I have never come
across them in the winter in masses, as one
finds the tabbies.   They do some harm, no
doubt, but I fancy they are chiefly scavengers
eating up decaying vegetation.   I found some
dead branches of a *Buddlœa globosa* with the
bark stripped clean by these little snails,
whereas none of the living branches were
touched by them in any way.   There are
endless varieties amongst these snails.   My
nephew Harry pointed many out to me,
amongst others one that had hairs or bristles
on its shell.

They are all very alert and difficult to
capture, as the least touch to the plant on
which they are feeding gives them the alarm,
and they fall directly to the ground, where
they are not easily afterwards found.   In the
winter I find immense quantities of their little
shells quite empty lying about, and I sometimes turn up a living one beneath dwarf

clumps of small plants, such as Sedums or Aubrietias.

I need not say that if the worms and snails are busy, the birds also are very hard at it foraging in every direction. The fish also seem very ravenous just now, a fisherman telling me that yesterday he had had eight runs from jack in about an hour and a half, though he only landed one.

In my last letter I meant to have told you about the seeds of the stork's-bill. These seeds have a long beak, which is spirally twisted ; there are bristles underneath it, and if one is slightly wetted and placed on the ground it will move along an inch or two. The spiral expands and uncurls itself with the damp, and this action, together with the little bristles, sends the thing along : a peculiar pro-perty of the seed, which allows it, as the weather changes from damp to dry, to move along on the ground a good distance from the parent plant.

The damp weather has caused plentiful

crops of fungi of every sort, mushrooms
being amongst others very plentiful just now.
A farmer told me a curious superstition, for

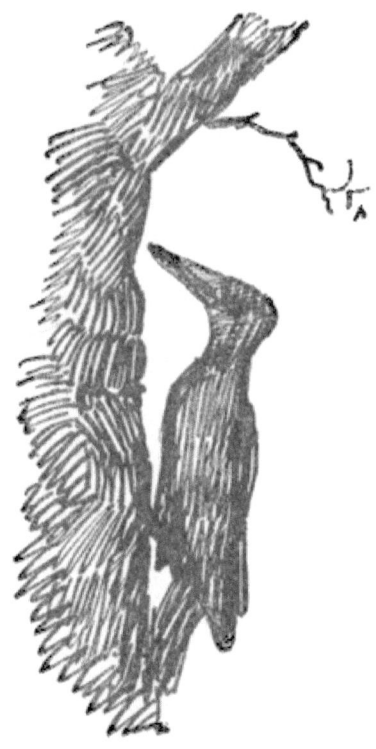

Green Woodpecker.

I can hardly believe it to be more, as to
mushrooms. It was that in any meadow
where an entire animal was placed mush-

rooms were sure to spring up, pointing to
a field of his which had never had mushrooms before in it until this year, when
several prize rams had been placed in it.
Certainly there was a fine crop in it when he
showed me the field. I have known other
country people who hold to the same
idea.

We had a visit from a large green woodpecker this morning. He comes to our sycamore tree pretty regularly once a year at about
the same season. He goes very carefully
over the tree, no doubt clearing it of many
little insects that lurk behind the flakes of the
bark. He leaves quite a litter of little bits of
bark beneath on the lawn after he has gone.
This bird seems to pick up something from
the grass itself at times. It is a very handsome bird, with a very pronounced neck, short
tail, and exquisite crimson crest. My little
scribble is done from recollection.

I had a charming letter from Hook the
other day. I sent him some time ago clumps

of flowering rushes and arrow-heads for his ponds. He tells me they are thriving well, and offers to send me some of his old-fashioned perennials in return.

G. D. L.

LETTER XIV

13th November 1886.

DEAR MARCO—The observations you
made in the country on the different ways
that leaves receive rain-drops interested me
greatly. You say you found that smooth and
shiny-surfaced leaves retained the little beads
of wet for a long time, but that the dull-surfaced ones appeared to dry up very soon. I
confess I have never paid attention to this
fact, and am at a loss to account for it; possibly
the dull-surfaced leaves absorb the rain a
great deal as it falls, like blotting-paper, the
plant drinking in the moisture through its
pores, whereas the shiny ones, being more

waterproof, retain the rain-drops until they
are dispersed by evaporation. There are
many plants with beautiful, dull, bloom-like
surfaces on their leaves, like the cabbage, the
columbine, or the nasturtium, which seem to
be to a great extent waterproof. On these
the drops of rain accumulate and form brilliant
globules of water, though I cannot see the
possible advantage this arrangement affords
the plant.

As to the rain, we have been in a state of
sop here for some time. The river has risen,
and everything looks sodden and miserable.
I actually did nothing in my garden for two
whole days. Yesterday, however, I · gave
some long-promised allowances of manure to
one or two plants and made them snug for
the winter, and in turning over the heaps I
disturbed an enormous fat toad, which I suppose had there taken up his winter quarters.
I have two toads in my greenhouse. They
are most useful, keeping the place quite free
from woodlice, earwigs, ants, etc. Frogs,

too, in a garden do much good in the same way, and should never be destroyed; they are invaluable in a strawberry-bed.   I think you, dear Marco, with your sense of the quaint and grotesque, would greatly delight in a tame

Toad, drawn from life.

toad as a pet.   It is a dignified-looking creature.   It breathes through two little pin-holes for nostrils.   Its mouth is wide; few insects escape it when once seized by the lightning dart of the tongue.   It scratches a hole in the ground, in which it sits with its head and shoulders out, or ensconces itself

beneath the cover of some thick-growing
dwarf plant. The great characteristic of the
creature is its remarkable motionless waiting-
power.

I am at a loss to account for the numbers
of frogs and toads in my garden, as I have no
stagnant pools or ponds in which these creatures pass the first stage of their existence;
and I can hardly believe the young tadpoles
could exist at all in the river itself, as, to say
nothing of the fish eating them, the floods
would inevitably sweep away any spawn that
was placed in it. Toads and frogs have a
power of exuding some sort of poison from
their bodies. This is done as a protection
from animals of prey. Dogs or cats will play
with frogs or toads with their paws, giving
them pats, but avoid taking them in their
mouths, drawing back from them suddenly
in a curious way. Frogs have to keep
themselves moist to be well, and they
carry a little supply of water in a pouch.
When suddenly attacked they discharge

this, no doubt to lighten themselves for jumping.

Shakespeare, as usual, is right in describing the

> Toad, that under the cold stone,
> Days and nights hast thirty-one
> Sweltered venom sleeping got,

as toads do swelter venom, and can easily exist thirty-one days beneath stones without food; but the old and oft-repeated idea that they could exist in perfect seclusion for almost an indefinite period was set at rest long ago by Dr. Buckland. He prepared a number of stones of different sorts and had small cavities made in them, in which toads, after having been weighed, were placed ; they were closed up with glass, cemented down, and then buried ; at the end of a year a few were still alive, and in one or two instances where the cementing had been insecurely done they had actually increased in weight, having no doubt partaken of sundry small insects which had penetrated into their cells; but at the end of the second year none had survived, and in those cases where the fastening was not quite perfect the toad itself had been devoured by insects of some sort.

Toads, I imagine, wander about at night, and feed chiefly then, and the numbers of flattened dead ones that are seen in country roads in the summer time are no doubt unfortunate toads which have been run over or trodden on during their night prowls. I send you a sketch I made from one of the toads in my greenhouse; he has now disappeared for the winter, but in the summer I feed him for the amusement of my friends. I place a woodlouse near him; he takes no notice of a dead one, and never attacks a living one as long as it is perfectly still, but the instant it moves he darts out his long tongue, on the end of which the creature disappears down his throat with an instantaneous rapidity that is quite startling, his mouth shutting with a slight click, and his eyes giving a sort of roll of satisfaction as the thing is swallowed.[1]

G. D. L.

[1] An Oxford friend tells me of a curious name for woodlice current in Oxfordshire, namely, "God Almighty's pigs." T. Tims, the Varsity bargeman, informed my friend that his mother cured him of whooping-cough by giving him fried woodlice ground to powder, and he called them by the above extraordinary name.

LETTER XV

27th November 1886.

DEAR MARCO— Different birds regard
man and his doings in very different ways;
for instance, swallows always seem to me
to ignore the existence of man altogether,
apparently far too much occupied in their
own business to take any notice of him. If
they find any buildings that are suitable for
their nests, they fearlessly and persistently
build there, quite unmindful of the movements and doings of the human owner. When
interfered with they appear bothered and
surprised, but if let alone they testify no
gratitude, but pursue their incessant business
of fly-catching. They no doubt are aware

that their time is short, their stay a mere
visit, and have not a moment to lose therefore. They likewise take little or no notice of
other birds, and their apparent boldness arises
chiefly from the reckless sense of security that
their exquisite power of flight gives them.

Very different is the sweet sociability and
confiding friendship with which the robin
treats us, or the impudent and time-serving
cupboard love of the sparrow. You can
scarcely take your hoe in your hand for
weeding purposes on an autumnal morning
before a robin sees you, and alighting on the
nearest branch gives forth the sweetest little
conciliating song in the world. Sure I am he
does this to win your favour, for if you talk
to him he answers and testifies his friendship
with sundry nods and bobs.

The sparrow is likewise very much alive
to your presence ; he, however, retreats before
you, though never very far away, dodging
about and keeping his eye on you much as a
street boy does when disturbed in a game of

doubtful propriety. The sparrow is bold,
but he knows that he is only tolerated, and
trusts more to his own artfulness than to
your favour.

The blackbird is proud and vain, and
almost resents the intrusion of man into his
hunting-grounds. He is a grand seignior
amongst other birds, and drives them before
him when able to do so ; you can almost
hear him say, " Go away, little birds, go
away." Blackbirds are very jealous of one
another, and are perpetually driving one
another away. I have to take a stick to
scare him from the gooseberry bushes, and
when I have caught one under the straw-
berry-nets it will as often as not show fight
and peck at my fingers.

Thrushes approximate far more to the
robins in sweetness of disposition, though far
shyer, and never addressing you individually
with their song, as does the robin.

The starling cares little for man. He is
not afraid of him, and takes advantage of his

outbuildings if desirable, making what use he can of the garden, its trees and sheds ; but all the starling's affection is for his own comrades, and this seems to last all the year round. Tomtits are the happiest little birds imaginable, and frequent man's neighbourhood freely ; too busy and active to think of life and its troubles, their little livers are never out of order, and as they have few enemies, they flit from branch to branch, any side up and upside down, generally in pairs, chirping their little shrill song all the while ; this little song, I have no doubt, is to signal to their mates their whereabouts. You may see all these birds very close in the winter if you feed them, but it is very sad to think that the robin is the only one which really cares for your friendship.

I hope to see you on the 1st, and don't forget to bring "Grandpapa Marco and his baby,"[1] I must have it.

G. D. L.

---

[1] A photograph of Mr. Marks with his first grandchild on his lap.

LETTER XVI

9th January 1887.

DEAR MARCO—The day before Christmas day I took my American cousins, who were spending Christmas with us, over to see Ewelme. I found old Clark still alive in his bed ; he is quite the last of the old people in the almshouse whom you would remember, and he quite well remembered Mr. Marks. He has been married twice since you knew him ; there are always weddings going on in the almshouses between the old widowers and widows. The weather was lovely on that day, and also on Christmas day, but the next night the storm began, and with it the

snow which played such havoc with the
telegraph poles on the railways; since then
the country round here has been entirely
covered with snow, and though it has thawed
occasionally the frost and snow returned
again directly.

I was very much amused, on the first
morning of the snow, with my cousin Gertrude
Leslie, who ran out into the deep snow in the
garden with delight, but suddenly exclaimed,
"Why, it's wet!" she being accustomed all
her life to the dry snow of America, in which
children can play without getting wet.

My garden is whiter than ever now. The
snow giants the children made on the lawn
look very formidable; one is an Elizabethan
lady with ruff and farthingale, a style of
costume which is easily rendered in snow.

The river is in flood, the meadows on its
banks being covered with frozen flood-water
and snow. The riverside folks here all
believe in the theory of what they call
ground-ice, which is, they say, ice that is

formed on the bottom of the river and which
rises to the top. They advance in proof of
this theory that the ice which floats down the
river at the beginning of a frost always has
weeds and their roots sticking in it, torn up,
as they think, from the river-bed. This ice
with the weeds in it is no doubt that which
gets frozen first at the edges of the river and
on the flooded sides, and which, if the river
rises afterwards at all, floats up, bringing with
it the tufts of weeds and their roots; in some
sense it might be called ground-ice, but it
does not come from the deep bottom of the
river, as I have often heard stated by farmers
and others. This ice is always seen about
the second day of the frost, after which, as
the river falls a little, no ice is seen for a day
or two, the stream running very strongly in
its natural bed, not allowing the formation of
ice; but after that, if the frost continues, large
sheets of ice begin to form in the eddies,
which gradually extend along the banks,
leaving but a very small channel in the

middle. Lastly, in extreme frosts, this channel
itself freezes and the moving waters are suddenly stilled ; where you have been accustomed so long to see the running stream day
by day, this stoppage has quite a startling
effect.

You may easily imagine that we feed the
birds every day.   They come in flocks:
thrushes, blackbirds, robins, chaffinches, tomtits, starlings, sparrows, and even rooks.
They share the chickens' food, scour the
waste-heaps, and search every possible nook
and cranny, as well as taking the scraps we
throw from the windows.   I go round with a
fork and turn over the manure-heaps and piles
of dead leaves, etc., turning out now and then
masses of hibernating snails, glued together
in lumps, from out-of-the-way hiding-places,
which I scatter in the open so as to supply
as much as possible the natural food of the
birds, and prevent them from getting dainty
by eating too much of meat scraps, etc.

The tits are the best off of all, for I hang

bones and fat by strings to the boughs of the bushes in front of our windows ; these bones are never left by the tits for many minutes all day long. The ox-eye or larger tit, the cole-tit, which is the smallest, and the tit-mouse : all three sorts come, and all seem well and active. There are no prettier birds in their plumage than these little fellows. They are very tame now, and I have often looked at them when they have been close up out-side the window, with my head equally close up inside, for quite a long time. These and the starlings are the only birds which don't seem to feel the cold much, keeping active and lively, and even singing at times. The thrushes and robins, on the other hand, seem to feel the cold worst of all, going about in a dejected manner with their feathers puffed up and a humpy back. The rooks hang about in a very artful way, perched on the branches of the sycamore and walnut trees, from whence they keep a very sharp look-out on the goings-on. Should a sparrow or star-

ling secure a rather large piece of food and
be making off with it, a rook will immediately
dash down and charge the bird, generally
causing it to drop the prize; the rook does
not, however, seize it at once, but after one or
two little circular movements alights near,
. walks up, and carries it off in triumph.   The
rook is a very light bird for the size of his
wings, which are more adapted for long
flights than manoeuvring in close quarters.
He is always a little awkward at alighting on
a branch or the ground; on the former he
executes several quaint movements with tail
and wings before he secures his balance, and
in approaching the latter he is very like a
small sailing-boat picking up its moorings,
having to check his way by a circular sort of
hover first, his feet hanging down all the
while in a curious way.

I hear the owls at night now, but am
utterly at a loss to account for the food they
find.   The moor-hens come up on the lawn
and even partake of the dole sometimes; they

look so very like hens feeding that their
name is easily accounted for ; they give continually a little sort of jerky flitch with their
wings when on shore, and are exceedingly
alert to danger of any sort.

There was a letter in the papers last
November from some gentleman who had
killed two gnats in his bedroom, and wrote
of it as a curious evidence of the mildness of
the weather ; the fact is, all through the
winter, the instant a thaw sets in swarms of
gnats and small flies may be seen in sheltered
corners near ivy or evergreen shrubs, flying
about calmly and composedly as if no such
thing as winter existed.   Gilbert White men-
tions this fact, and during the many curiously
intervening thaws which have occurred lately
I have noticed it repeatedly.   It has been
thawing up to 12 P.M. and freezing hard the
next morning sometimes, and at others a
bright frosty moonlight night has been
followed by warm thaw at daybreak.   Such,
dear Marco, is the mutability of our fickle

climate; would that the long frost of art patronage would give way sometimes likewise.

A solitary black-headed bunting has been the only strange visitor to us during this frost.

                                        G. D. L.

P.S.—As far as I can see the thrushes are the only birds that eat the snails that I turn out.

LETTER XVII

7*th March* 1887.

DEAR MARCO—You ask me what I think about the packing of birds in the autumn, etc. I always feel that it is a mistake to regard this as a partial or temporary phase in bird life, but rather that it is the ordinary social arrangement of most birds except those of prey, which is broken through during the breeding season and resumed again afterwards ; in short, I look upon it as their normal state. The old proverb has much truth in it which says, "Birds of a feather flock together," and surely it is no odd thing for them to do when we see not only beasts, fishes, and insects, but men also doing the same. Why should not birds be fond of each other's company, or take advantage of the safety that is found in numbers ? Your newspaper correspondent forgets that packing takes place in autumn, when food is plentiful, each species of bird naturally flocking to the places where its peculiar food most abounds, and when many birds of a partial migratory character naturally assemble for departure.

The young broods, when their first home is broken up, most naturally keep together with their seniors, so as to take advantage of their experience. During their infancy they have to be fed on a very different diet to that which is afterwards their usual food, and it is for this purpose that the parent birds, when the breeding season comes round, separate and break up their usual societies, and each selects some suitable locality in which the peculiar and necessary food abounds. I have seen many thousands of larks flying overhead in one long continual stream, taking a south-westerly course at the

commencement of a hard frost, and have no
doubt these birds feed in flocks, except during
the breeding season, when they separate, and
each half acre of cultivated land has its pair
of larks and nest upon it.   In winter, during
frosts, food for the birds is only found in
isolated   spots,   towards   which   they   are
naturally drawn together for self-preserva-
tion.   A freshly ploughed or manured field,
a disturbed manure-heap, a flooded meadow,
or the water-course of a spring that does not
freeze, is sure to attract a flock or pack of
birds.

Then again the advantages of safety are
obvious.   Surprise from enemies is almost
impossible to a large flock of birds, each
member of which can feed at leisure in a way
that the solitary bird dares not trust itself
to do.

The only difficulty I find is in the case of
the many birds that do not apparently pack.
In the case of birds of prey it is easily under-
stood, as neither beasts nor fish of prey assort

together ; their whole manner and method of feeding is different, and nature seems to have inflicted a penalty, so to speak, on them of solitude and isolation ; were it not so, they would naturally soon cause their own famine. I believe woodpeckers and several other species do not pack, but they may almost be considered as belonging to the birds of prey. Robins do not pack, but in this case I believe the robin may be considered as having almost become domesticated, so connected with man and his surroundings is he. In his case there is no necessity for packing, in the ordinary sense of the word. There is a little family flock or tribe of robins attached to each cottage-garden and orchard, to which they cling all the year round. They become there almost as domesticated as the dogs and cats. They love the place as a cat loves hers, and should their landlord be of a kindly disposition, will sing to him and bob their heads with a winning grace that quite resembles the wag of the tail or lick of the hand that the dog

gives his master. There is no necessity for
the change of their abode ; the food they find
there suits them at all seasons, and is equally
adapted for the young fledgling as the full-
grown bird. In the winter too there are
few people indeed, even amongst the
humblest, that do not at least throw food to
the robin.

The robin has a character for pugnacity,
especially in the breeding season, and I have
often picked up dead ones in the early spring,
which I am led to believe are aged gentlemen
which have succumbed to more youthful
rivals, or may have died a natural death from
old age. I do not think that they are naturally quarrelsome ; but it stands to reason, as
they will not leave their old homesteads the
accommodation must become limited, and
either the young or old birds must give way
some time or another. I suppose the old
birds hold their ground for as many years as
they can, driving farther afield the younger,
but at last have to give way. In the autumn

they seem friendly enough, each having his allotment of one or two apple trees and some old palings or other; you will easily after a bit recognise individual robins in your garden, each haunting his own domain. When a robin enters the room of a house it does not flutter about in alarm as other birds do, but will fly and perch about comparatively at its ease, and sometimes almost refuses to quit. My brother Bradford tells me that in India they have a pied robin, exactly like our robin in all things except its colour, which is black and white.

G. D. L.

I

LETTER XVIII

3rd February 1888.

I WAS reminded of you, my dear Marco, a short time back when I took my boy to Marlborough in the train through the Kennet Valley ; it recalled pleasant memories of our visit years ago to Ramsbury. The great number of birds of all sorts David and I saw from the carriage windows still further reminded me of you, and I felt ashamed at having so long neglected my correspondence with my old friend. The day we travelled was keen and frosty ; the river-meadows and marshlands alongside the railway swarmed

with birds of all sorts ; numberless plovers,
moorhens, coots, dabchicks, kingfishers, and
rooks afforded us great interest, and the sight
of a fine heron which rose up from a ditch
beneath us made us nearly forget the school-
ward journey we were taking. It is not
often one looks down on the huge, gray, expanded wings of a heron as we did, more
like some old gray umbrella than anything
else.

About Christmas time I saw two gulls
flying over the river, and kingfishers have
daily frequented the campshedding during
the winter. The tits at their hanging bones
have been as amusing as ever. Whenever
the frost gave way the thrushes and starlings
sang, giving us foretastes of the coming spring.
Starlings, I believe, from their habits of fre-
quenting their old nests or other places of
refuge in the winter, are very much infested
with vermin, and never tire of washing themselves even in the coldest day ; the energy
with which they shake themselves when thus

engaged being very characteristic of these lively birds.

About a week ago my nephew, Clayton Leslie, called my attention to the remains of a large jack which he found lying on the steps of my old boat-house. This old boat-house is hardly ever used now, and is in a secluded part of the garden. The remains in question consisted of the head and part of the tail of what must have been at least a 6 lb. fish ; all the rest was apparently eaten away by some creature. The fish was quite fresh, and even bleeding a little, and could not have long been there. We came to the conclusion that it was the work of an otter for many reasons. In the first place, no other creature except a cat would have eaten such raw fish ; but apart from the fact that no cat could have caught or mastered so large a fish, the only entrance to this boat-house, the door being shut, was from the water, whilst the step on which the remains lay was submerged with water about an inch or more ; a cat would

THE OLD BOAT-HOUSE AT RIVERSIDE.

To face page 116.

never have eaten it in so wet a place; besides, the quantity eaten was enough for three cats. The following day we found nothing but the head left, and, on further inspection, several other jacks' heads at the bottom of the water close by. The evidence as to its having been the work of an otter seemed very conclusive, especially as I have heard repeated rumours of the existence of these creatures in the neighbourhood. These beasts are very partial to jack, and are nocturnal in their predatory expeditions, probably pouncing on their prey in the early hours of the morning; anyhow, an otter must have found in my boat-house a very convenient landing-place and slaughter-house for the fish he caught. Many letters have appeared lately in the *Field* as to the increase of otters on the Thames, and complaints made of the new law forbidding any sort of shooting or trapping on its banks. There was a report once here that a pack of otter-hounds from Thame were coming over to hunt here, but

it was but an idle rumour. I believe so
large a river could not be managed by the
dogs.

My American cousins have sent me lately
a box containing two curiosities, one of which
is the body of a bee-bird, the smallest bird
known : it is a humming-bird, but not often
seen in the stuffed specimens in cases, as its
colours are but humble and quiet.

The Bee-bird.

I have made a little drawing of it for you
the exact size of nature. I remember my
father once mistaking a hawk - moth for a
humming-bird in our garden ; he was greatly
excited about it and quite sure it must have
been a bird which had somehow crossed the
Atlantic; and the sight of this minute bee-bird
explains to me now how he came to be
mistaken, as it would certainly with wings

extended be no bigger than some of the hawk-moths. The ordinary humming-bird moth seems to me to be too small, but some of the larger hawk-moths might well pass for this bird. The other curiosity is called "a resurrection plant," and is some sort of large lichen or spleenwort from Colorado. It looked when it arrived just like a piece of dried-up coarse moss, all curled up and of a grayish brown colour, with a few hairy roots, and was apparently quite dead ; but on putting it in a saucer of water in a day or two it slowly uncurled itself and opened out into a very beautiful fern-like moss or spleenwort, of a fresh deep green colour, with extremely well-defined and elegantly cut fronds. As long as I kept it moist it remained uncurled and expanded, but on allowing it to dry up it once more relapsed into the shapeless mass it was when it came to me. Since then it has revived and died three times for the amusement of my friends and children, and is at present alive again.

I do not know whether you ever heard of
the patriotic movement our grandfathers made
in the matter of planting walnut trees.   Most
of the large walnut trees about here are of
the same size and age, and were planted about
the time of the battle of Waterloo.   It appears
that there had been great destruction amongst
these trees throughout the southern counties
for the sake of their wood for gun-stocks, so
our fathers planted these trees to supply the
deficiencies.   I had this from a countryman
who remembered his father telling him of it,
à propos of a tree, at Aston Tyrold, which is
now just such a one as my large tree.   The
walnut is not a very long-lived tree, judging
from this ; I should say few live much over a
hundred years.   I know a row of these trees
near the Swan at Shillingford, which the last
landlord there told me he had himself planted,
that are now forty or forty-five years old; they
are fine large trees, but not as large and grand
as the Waterloo heroes that abound in the
Berkshire villages.

Write soon, so as to encourage me in my resumed correspondence.

G. D. L.

P.S.—This last winter we had a visit from a travelling theatre ; it was a sort of barn-like

The Star Theatre during a Flood.

structure erected in the meadow opposite our house. We went once to see the performance ; it was not half bad. The house was warmed with a brazier of coke, and the prices varied from one penny to sixpence. During the floods it was shut up and looked very desolate; I send you a sketch from recollection of it at this period. Whilst here the wife of the manager had a baby; it was born in a travelling van that accompanied the theatre, and was christened in Crowmarsh Church and named "Wallingford."

LETTER XIX

5th October 1888.

DEAR MARCO—Again I have neglected
you for a great while in an entirely inexcus-
able way. To-day I found a letter that I
began to you in May last which I left un-
finished ; I enclose it, to in some measure fill
up the gap.

This last summer has been a curiously
inclement one, the fruit scarcely ripening at
at all, hardly an apple fit to eat without cook-
ing it, gooseberries and strawberries being
the only things that did well. I had a mag-
nificent show of apricots on the south wall of

a malt-house, which grew large, and coloured
on the one side of the loveliest rosy orange,
whilst the side against the wall never ripened
at all, the sunny sides going rotten long first.
I made a little jam and some puddings from
them, and that was all.   On the other hand,
we have never been without the most delicious
peas all through the summer, and still have
nice dishes of them every other day; the
rainy weather having kept them growing and
bearing, and they have all the richness and
softness imaginable.

One or two sharp frosts have already
taken place.   The rooks have begun to carry
off the walnuts (by the bye a rook with a
bright new walnut in his beak against a blue
sky is a thing to be painted, the walnut in the
sun looking like gold).   The song of the tomtits and robins, and the chatter and conversation of the starlings, remind one of the
approach of winter.

It has been a terribly hard time for our poor
farmers, much corn and oats being still unripe.

The hay harvest was an utter failure, the hay
looking more like manure on the fields than
hay ; some I was told had lain on the ground
for five weeks.   It has been, as I daresay
you know too well, a wretched year for the
arts.   Nevertheless, young people seem irre-
pressible, weddings and births being numerous around this neighbourhood.   My brother
Robert's youngest boy will marry my neighbour Mr. Hayllar's daughter next Tuesday,
starting for India with her soon afterwards.

[Here follows the May fragment.]

There are few things more sad and em-
barrassing to any one fond of birds than when
in the spring time or early summer a young
thrush or starling, just out of the nest for the
first time, is brought to you by your children
as a great prize.   This happens very frequently to me at this season, when five or six
of these large-mouthed, short-tailed, weak-
legged things are continually being suddenly

launched from their nests into the open.
They get scattered about in the garden and
shrubberies in the most aggravating manner,
their parents having all their work cut out to
defend and provide for them, many sooner or
later falling victims to cats, rats, weasels, or
boys.   When brought to you by the children
it is hard to know what to do ; it seems cruel
to abandon them altogether, and restoring
them to their parents is a much more difficult
thing to do than most people would imagine.
I generally take them into the greenhouse,
where at any rate the cats cannot get at them,
and endeavour to keep them alive for a time
until they have sufficient wing-power to shift for
themselves.   Feeding them is an endless task.
Every hour I give them worms, for which
food their beaks and throats are wonderfully
adapted, the tongues having barbs to them
which render the escape of the worms impossible ; but it is fifty to one that on visiting the
bird on the second morning it will be found
stretched out stiff and ugly on the ground

dead. I believe these worms are not in a proper state for the crops of the birds, as I have noticed thrushes, after having extracted a worm from the ground, do not carry it away immediately, but peck it about, possibly separating some part that is unwholesome, or else giving it a sort of mastication which renders it digestible. Some worms after extraction are abandoned by the birds without any apparent reason.

There is evidently a large percentage of loss in every brood; I think it is unlikely that more than two birds out of each brood survive to maturity. Rooks, magpies, and jackdaws often help themselves to young half-fledged birds from the nests; but the young of thrushes and blackbirds are chiefly decimated when they first quit the nests, being exceedingly helpless and awkward on the ground. Our cat and my neighbour's one are very much on the alert at this season, and no doubt in wilder places stoats and weasels are wide awake just now; anyhow, I curse my stars when the children bring me one of these helpless waifs and strays, knowing from repeated experiences the futility of attempting to hand-rear them.

The painful alarm cry "chig, chig, chigg," rapidly repeated every now and then, announces the fact that a prize has been secured by the cat; feathers, bits of wings, etc., found lying about tell the same tale.

About a fortnight ago I saw four terns hawking over the river for fish. It was in the afternoon during windy, sunny weather, and this time I paid particular attention to their tails, which undoubtedly were distinctly forked.

[*Fragment ends.*]

5th October 1888.

Forked tails remind me that the swallow's tail is frequently drawn wrongly by artists. The fact that swallows have forked tails is almost always too much insisted on ; whether the bird is meant to be flying at full speed or perched at rest the tail is generally shown forked in far too pronounced a manner. When a swallow is flying swiftly forward the tail is closed, and when at rest or perched the tail is likewise closed, presenting really two straight lines which almost close together. In the case of the house martin or sand martin, if the tail is fully expanded the base line of the fan is nearly straight; in the tail of the chimney swallow the two outside feathers are much the longest.

A swallow uses his tail to check his flight, expanding it entirely in stopping, and partially in order to slack or turn, but at full speed it is straight as an arrow. The tail acts both as a rudder and a brake. At rest it is never forked out; the muscles that spread the tail are extensors and require an effort to keep them in action, just as in our hands we have to exert power to keep the fingers stretched out, but the moment the hand is at rest the fingers close and curl up slightly.

Numbers of swallows settle every morning

K

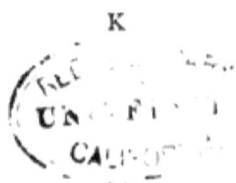

now on the coping above my bedroom
window, enjoying the morning sun ; and I can
see their tails and the ends of their wings
projecting below, very like little more than
three straight lines, as in the sketch, the

Swallow Tails and Wing-tips.

centre line being the tail and the outer lines
the wings.

Even Bewick has represented his swallow
with too forked a tail considering that the
bird is perched. The representation of the
forked tail, without regard to what the bird
is intended to be doing, has become, through
long custom, a conventionality.

G. D. L.

LETTER XX

7th December 1888.

DEAR MARCO—Extra length of the strong
outside feathers of the tail, which causes us
to call it forked, is mostly found in the case
of birds of very rapid flight, such as hawks,
terns, swallows, fern-owls, or humming-birds ;
and in some cases these outside feathers have
a slight curve outwards which still further
increases their brake or steering power.
Kingfishers would be generally considered as
very rapid fliers, and their tails are certainly
short and not forked ; but I am inclined to
think their straight arrow-like flight is not
so very rapid as we imagine. It has been
compared to a meteor, but plenty of time is

afforded to mark well both the shape and
varied colour of the bird. I believe that the
extreme suddenness of the pleasure we enjoy
at the beauty of the sight causes us uncon-
sciously to exaggerate the shortness of the
period of enjoyment.

The mild weather, which has been so
remarkable, still continues. The various
anomalies amongst the flowers in my garden
are very curious, I might even term them
anachronisms. Thus I have Christmas roses
and sweet peas in bloom at the same time.
I picked quite a nice bunch of these latter
two days ago. Primroses, polyanthuses,
violets, and pansies are flowering freely. Out-
door chrysanthemums still go on. Several
strawberry plants are in full bloom ; even
fruit in some cases being quite large, though
green. I picked one or two blooms of the
bloody cranesbill and of the sweet-scented
evening primrose, *Œnothera odorata.* Tea
roses keep throwing out buds and flowers.
A blue perennial lupin has been blooming

strongly all the last month, and last week I
had a poppy in flower. There are also in
bloom periwinkles, aubrietia, allysum, mari-
golds (the potherb, the common corn, and the
African), torchflowers, and winter jasmine.
At the same time the crocuses and spring
bulbs are all showing up through the ground,
whilst several asters, or Michaelmas daisies,
are still in flower. To-day the sky is cloudless and the temperature that of summer.
Blackbirds, thrushes, and larks sing nearly
all day long, and this is the seventh of
December.

I forgot in my last letter to mention a
rather curious phenomenon that occurred
sometime this autumn (I am sorry I have lost
the date); namely, that one fine night the
sheep at all the different farms in this
neighbourhood, with very few exceptions,
broke out of their folds and were found the
next morning at considerable distances. The
tract of land in which this took place extended
on both sides of the river between here and

Abingdon, a distance of over nine miles. The
farmers were quite at a loss to account for it.
That it was the work of some mischievous
person is impossible, owing to the vast extent
of the phenomenon, whilst the simultaneous-
ness of its occurrence, which was verified in
many instances, precludes the idea that it
could have been the work of a wandering dog
or other animal. The sheep were not in any
case injured, and had in most instances simply
jumped the folds. It was generally believed
to have been occasioned by a slight earth-
quake, though, as no human being noticed
any shock, it is curious that the sheep should
have felt it.

I was sorry I saw so little of you at the
two last R.A. meetings, and as I cannot
come up on the 10th to hear the President, I
am afraid I shall not see my old friend again
this year; so pray write and tell me how
things in general, and you in particular, are
going on. My picture is at present in a state
of jib, owing to a child's head in it which I

cannot get right, and which I feel must be done before I can go on with the rest of the work.   I live in hope, however.

G. D. L.

P.S.—Just as I was sending this to post I came across the enclosed cutting from a local paper about the stampede of sheep.   It gives the date and some further particulars.

THE STAMPEDE OF SHEEP.—We are informed that the phenomenon which occurred during the night of the 3rd November was experienced to a considerable extent in the district west of Abingdon, as well as in those parishes lying to the south and south-east previously mentioned.   On Mr. T. Floyd's farm, at Frilford, a wall fell in three places, and the sheep, as well as those at Appleton and other parishes, took fright in the same extraordinary manner as did the flocks of the whole country side, ranging, it is said, from Faringdon to Reading.

LETTER XXI

4th March 1889.

DEAR MARCO—I began a letter to you
some four weeks ago, but it is not worth
sending; it spoke of the lovely mildness of
the weather, and how the spring flowers were
all coming into bloom, and now as you know
the old Candlemas saying has come true.
My poor crocuses are sadly put to it, the sun
tempting them out by day, whilst the frost
smites them down by night.   Everything has
been in a wretched condition of blighted
existence for the last ten days.

Crocus bulbs have an awkward way of

getting pushed up out of the ground, becoming often thus the prey of mice or birds.
This mischief is done mostly by the frost,
which raises the ground with the crocus
clumps altogether, then when the thaw and
rain come the soil gets washed down leaving
the crocuses propped up by their roots, which
lengthen even during the frost.   Thus in
old established clumps (which are always the
finest in effect) many weakly bulbs get
crowded out on to the surface.   The loss is,
however, amply made up for by the numbers
of young seedlings which spring up around
the parent clump.

I hear that *the* professor does not like
gathering flowers, or to have them, when
gathered, in the house, except for special study
purposes ; and though I cannot altogether
agree with him as to this, I think, certainly,
the way to enjoy flowers best is to see them
growing ; no crocuses picked can compare in
beauty and interest to a fine old clump in the
ground.   But still, on the other hand, in this

cold, changeable weather it seems almost a
kindness to gather little precocious primroses
and scillas and bring them indoors out of the
blighting frost ; I have some which my little
girl gathered in a mug in the greenhouse,
which have been blooming away for more
than a week, during which their companions
in the garden have nearly perished with the
cold.

We have lately a new pleasure, in the
shape of a kitten, added to our establish-
ment. Our old house-cat, who is celebrated
for his amiability, was rather jealous at first,
and resented the kitten's endeavours to play
with it ; but as he is too kind to hurt it, he
generally utters a whine and leaves the room
when the kitten approaches him.

I have been theorising on the effect of
what we call fire in a cat's eyes, I mean when
the whole eye assumes that luminous red
light which is often noticed ; and I feel pretty
sure, from various observations, that cats
have either the voluntary or involuntary

power of causing this effect when thinking of,
or eager for food, or intent on capturing their
prey. Our kitten's eyes shine thus when
about to spring at anything in play, and both
our kitten's and cat's eyes thus shine when
food is presented to them. The effect is not,
however, noticed unless the creature is in
shade, and then only at certain angles. As
a cat generally approaches its prey from
under cover and in shade, I believe the two
bright red spots of light serve to attract the
curiosity of the victim so as to divert its
attention for a few fatal moments, or may
perhaps hypnotise it in some way, which pro-
ceeding has led to the idea of the power of
fascination belonging to the cat tribe.

I saw lately at a school-treat a remarkable
instance of this same luminous fire-light
phenomenon in the eyes of a little girl: she
had rather large gray eyes, which I remarked
glowed light as a cat's eyes as she stood
waiting, in rather a shady corner, her turn
for the buns and oranges which were being

distributed.   Is it possible it was the thoughts
of food that acted on her eyes, as I suppose
they do in the case of cats ?

I daresay you remember that many of the
little children we used to paint from when
we were at Benson called themselves "love
children."   "Please, sir, she's a love child."
Married women amongst the labouring classes
around here have sometimes one or two
illegitimate children by their husbands as
well as legitimate ones ; they speak of these
quite complacently as born in "lovelock," as
distinct from "wedlock."   This rural im-
morality seems to me to smack a good deal
of the old mediæval days when houses had
only one sleeping-room for all comers, as in
the days of Chaucer.   I well remember
sleeping in a cottage in Warwickshire in 'a
room with only a curtain drawn between my
bed and another part of the room where my
host and his wife slept ; and I believe a good
deal of this sort of thing goes on still in
rough country lodgings.

The fact that the leaves of holly bushes
are not armed with spines when they grow
on the parts above the reach of cattle has
been noticed by naturalists. I have observed
the same sort of thing, or something analogous
to it, in ivy, the lower leaves of which, and
those close to the stems, are generally pointed
and angular, whilst the leaves that grow up
high and extend out into the air are rounded ;
and as the cattle-feeding theory could have
nothing to do with this arrangement in ivy
leaves, I am a little inclined to doubt the
evolutionary theory as regards the holly.

I am still very dissatisfied with one of my
pictures, and begin to think that I have chosen
a subject with which I do not feel sufficient
sympathy, as I somehow do not work at it
with the proper enthusiasm. It is very
mortifying, as I have wasted so much time
over it trying all sorts of arrangements. I
can never make a success unless I can see
my picture before commencing it, and in this
case I have been trying to build up a picture

from my intellect rather than from my heart.
I am quite sure the heart is the only true guide.
It is very sad at my age, but I suppose one
lives and learns even after fifty. You, my
dear Marco, have always succeeded best
when your subjects have dropped as it were
from the clouds to you. Pictures that run
straight off the reel at once, heart and hand
going together in the work, are always the
best a man produces. There is a lot of
fluking in the art, and I am quite sure when
we once begin to try and *make* a good picture
it is all up with it. The picture ought to
make itself if once rightly conceived. Possibly as we get older our inspirations grow
less frequent ; anyhow, let us not grow sour
and crapulous.

I long for an hour's chat with you in my
own studio, or in yours, as in old days, when
a visit from one of us to the other often cleared
away a lot of cobwebs of gloom and despondency. Scarcely a D.B. ending, but forgive
and believe me, ever yours,   G. D. L.

LETTER XXII

10th April 1889.

DEAR MARCO—Only a short letter to describe a pretty sight we enjoyed here on the 22nd of last month, and which I somehow forgot to tell you about when in town. It was at lunch time, 1.30, when my boy Peter called my attention to a flight of beautiful white birds over the meadows opposite our house. At first I took them for a return of the terns, but very soon discovered my mistake; for their flight was totally different in character and their tails were not forked. I have no doubt but that these were gulls, probably the small black-headed gull, which at this time of the year loses his black cap; at any rate, they had white heads. I counted

them twice, and made out forty at one time
and thirty-nine another ; my wife also made
them thirty-nine.

The river had been in rather high flood,
and though it was running off, there still was
a good deal of shallow water left over the
meadows. The gulls flew round and round
in a flock and settled on the meadow by the
flood-water. The sun was shining brightly,
and the gulls, mixed up with the black rooks,
which were also feeding by the shallow water,
looked excessively pretty. The rooks resented the intrusion of the strangers ; but the
gulls took little notice of the rooks' attacks,
merely shifting farther into the water out of
their way. I went out to my boat-house and
had a good look at them with my field-glass.

These gulls come inland to breed about
this time, and were no doubt attracted by the
floods to the river. I have before now seen
one or two gulls occasionally on the river,
but so large a flock as this never.

The weather has been so wet and bad

since we came back from town, that I cannot
sow my annuals, varnish my boat, or ride on
my tricycle—all which things I had proposed
to do at this period.   G. D. L.

LETTER XXIII

27th June 1889.

DEAR MARCO—The weather has been
wonderfully fine since Whitsuntide, the
flowers in my garden more beautiful than I
ever saw them before, but the warfare with
snails and weeds has been a severe struggle,
and only partially successful. Thanks to the
birds, we have not suffered from the plague
of caterpillars which I hear has been so pre-
valent in places this year. My strawberries
are very large and fine, and as they and the
roses are just now in full swing, I have given
up all thoughts of coming up to the soirée at
the Academy.

I have begun a garden picture, but at
present am at a loss for models, as my
favourite one has unfortunately engaged herself at the R.A. school, and the local girls
and young ladies about here are of little use,
except for the head, as they can neither take
nor keep a pose.   You know well my im-
patience, and will sympathise with me.   To
pass the time away, I went for a little excur-
sion with my wife last week : first to Marlborough to see my boys, and then across
what to me was unknown land, through
Swindon to Cheltenham, where Alice is at
the college.   After that we came back to
Cirencester, with which I was much delighted ; the large church there is very fine
indeed, and full of good bits, notably a wall-
painting of St. Christopher and the Child
Christ.   The masonry of the tower, with its
huge buttresses at its base spreading out like
the great roots of an elm or poplar, is most
interesting, the stones being worked diagon-
ally ; it looks to me as though it was origin-

ally built like this, and the tower has quite
the expression of having grown so like a
huge tree.

From Cirencester we drove over to Fairford, about eight miles, through very pretty
country, the watershed of the Thames.
I had never seen the Fairford windows,
and confess to being a little disappointed
with them, though much very fine colour
and quaint design abounds. I don't think
they deserve quite the praise that has been
bestowed upon them, and see little in them
to authorise the idea that they may be partly
designed by Albert Durer. The next day
we went to Lechlade, a place I knew, but
none the less glad to see again. The river
there is of course small and very much
twisted about, but has a wild beauty of its
own ; the cottages in the neighbourhood are
stone built, with exquisite roofs of flat stones,
lovely with moss and lichen.

We arrived at Lechlade in the afternoon,
and remembering on a former visit the old

Elizabethan manor-house at Kelmscott, in
which Rossetti formerly lived, and which is
now the country abode of W. Morris, I
persuaded my wife, though somewhat tired,
to walk over there. I had underestimated
the distance (some three miles), and was
rather hazy about the way, having only
reached it before from my boat on the river.
We only met one person the whole way,
but as he was the postman he was quite
sufficient.

When we got there I was rather sorry
to find that the trees and ivy had grown
so round the somewhat high garden walls
that very little beyond the gables of the
house were visible. My wife, more venture-
some, tried the garden-door, which was
open, and peeped in, and had a glimpse of
the old house and quaint garden ; I strolled
round to the back part through a sort of
farmyard, the place looking quite deserted
and silent. I imagined no one was there at
the time, when I was suddenly aware of

Morris's head leaning out of an upper
window ; of course explanations ensued, and
he came down at once, in the kindest
manner, brought us in, and showed us over
the whole place, which was well worth a
walk of double the distance to have seen.

I never saw an old house so lovingly and
tenderly fitted up and cared for as this one ;
the perfect taste and keeping of the furniture
and hangings, and the way in which the
original beauties of the house had been preserved was indeed a lesson to be remembered.
The window-seats had cushions in them, the
floors were beautifully clean, the old boards
by no means disguised or disfigured with
stain or varnish, with the right sort of mats
and carpets where wanted, some fine old
tapestry belonging to the house still hung on
the walls in one room, and the furniture
throughout was simple in character and not
overcrowded. That Morris's daughter herself also harmonised most gracefully with the
sweet place I need scarcely say. In the bed-

rooms were nice old fourpost bedsteads with
simple countrified chairs and tables, everything clean, cared for, and comfortable ; there
was throughout an utter absence of the over-
done modern aesthetic affectation. Morris
took us up into the attics, where he delighted
in descanting on the splendid old woodwork
displayed in the trussing and staying of the
roof - timbers. He had just finished his
supper, which, hungry as we were, looked
extremely good, and begged us to stay and
have some ; but as it was getting late, and I
had ordered chops at the inn, we had to
hurry off. We paid a visit to the garden,
which was kept up with the same skill and
taste ; the whole was fragrant with lavender
and the scent of the newly-clipped box
hedges ; the paths were very neat, and on
one hedge, a clipt yew, was the form of a
dragon, which Morris had amused himself
by gradually developing with the clippers.

Miss Morris gave my wife a rose of so
old and quaint a sort that I could give no

name to it; it had a bloom somewhat like a
monthly rose, only smaller and very sweet;
the foliage resembled that of the burnett rose,
which is, however, generally white; it may

Recollection of Kelmscott Rose.

have been a red burnett rose, but I never
saw one before like it, and believe it some
old-fashioned sort that has lingered on in
this old garden, possibly elsewhere obsolete.
Morris took us by a short cut across his
standing-crop of grass and bade us a most

friendly farewell at his boundary stile, and we hastened home, where we arrived exactly three-quarters of an hour late for our chops, which we enjoyed nevertheless exceedingly.

After supper my wife retired early, and I sat smoking alone in the large old oak-panelled room of the inn, used for country meetings and club dinners. The whole household were at rest, and I almost expected to see the ghost of Sophia Western or Parson Adams walk in. The new inn, as it is called, is a very good specimen of the George the Second period, just like Hogarth's interiors, and the old room I sat in had been altered very little; our little bedroom was entered through this room, and had one of those old black four-posters with dimity curtains which in old times hosts used to declare "had been slept in by the highest quality in the shire." No ghosts appeared, and we returned home the next day.

I have nothing much else to tell you at

present, unless it be that on Saturday evening last a poor horse got into the flam, or
muddy edge of the river, and was drowned
in some six inches of water during the night.
It belonged to a travelling pedlar of brushes
and brooms, who hawked these things about
in a cart ; he had paid sixpence for the horse's
keep in the meadow opposite our house, and
had what is termed hobbled it, *i.e.* tied one
of its fore legs to a hind one. The poor
thing, in trying to reach the water to drink,
stuck fast in the mud, fell with his head in
the water, and so was drowned. What
interested me most was the behaviour of the
other horses which were in the same field ;
they came down close to the dead one,
grunting and whinnying and pawing the
ground in a very curious way, seeming bent
on arousing the dead one.

The man was in an awkward predicament
with his cart and brooms. I need not say
that he valued the horse at a high figure,—
£20, I think,—and lost no time in sending

round the hat for subscriptions to buy a new one.

The cuckoo, which has been singing incessantly for the last eight weeks, has begun that absurd alteration in his notes which is a peculiarity of the bird ; he no longer says cuckoo, but cuck-cuckoo and cuckoo-cuck.

Farewell, dear Marco. I shall be at South Kensington on the 2nd and 3rd, but am afraid those are not the days you will be there. G. D. L.

2nd August 1889.

DEAR MARCO—You, I know, will sympathise with me in the rather mad journey
which I made two days ago, literally pot-
hunting, in the Midland counties. From
earliest childhood canal-boats have been to
me objects of love and interest, their pretty
cabins and quaint bright decorations especially delighting me; yet, strange to say, until
last week, I had never been inside one.
There was a very good specimen at the
wharf here last week, the woman on board
of which invited me to come aboard and see
the interior of the little cabin. I was perfectly astonished at the comfort, roominess,

and tidiness, but above all struck with the
immense amount of decoration which abounded
on every side ; each panel and cupboard-door

Rudder of a Canal-boat.   The shading is done heraldic to
indicate the colour.

had floral pieces and landscapes on it.   In
most of these boats the same style of conven-
tional, brightly-coloured decoration is found ;
a style which is exceedingly picturesque and
delightful, and which I believe to be one

that has survived to the present times very
little changed from mediæval days. The
various shapes, streaks, spots, etc., I imagine
to have a very close relation to the ancient
adornment of the galleys of our ancestors ;
there is a universally recurring yellow circle,
which I have little doubt is a survival of a
solar symbol.

On the deck of these cabins you may
perhaps have observed a large, brightly-
painted can ; this is called a deck-can, and
holds the drinking-water; the bargemen
replenish these cans during the journey
through high levels at favourite springs.
They hold about two gallons or rather more,
are usually painted green with a red band
round the centre, on which is the name of the
barge, the handles are bright red, and the
whole can profusely decorated with flowers,
etc. They have a broad, strong base, and
stand firmly ; there are little lids to the top
and to the spout to keep dust out. I never
saw these cans anywhere but on barges, and

had no idea where they were made; the
woman told me they got them at Measham,
in Leicestershire, and as I greatly longed to
possess one, with my usual impetuosity, I
looked up Measham in a Bradshaw, and

Deck-can.

started off for it the next day. The trains
were awkward, there being no less than six
junctions to be passed, and I had to spend
the night at Coventry, from whence the line
passes to Nuneaton, through that sort of
country the soil of which is chiefly composed

of cinders and brickbats : not the deep red
bricks of Berks or Kent, but dull, pale
abominations peculiar to the Midlands. From
Nuneaton to Measham the canal runs beside
the railway, going on to the coal districts.
I had only one hour to find the tinman at
Measham, but luckily came across him at once,
a Mr. Malcolm ; he was an intelligent and
clever workman, and possessed quite a little
manufactory, in which he made these cans
and other things used by the bargees—dippers,
and those tin pots for the horses' food, amongst
others.   He had no can ready, having sold
the last the day before, but I commissioned
him to make one, which he said he would
pack and send ; it was to cost five shillings
for the can, and the flowering would be half
a crown more, but it will be on the whole a
rather expensive can to me.   The flowering is
done by some local artist, who may have learnt
his art at some of the potteries in the district,
where the old-fashioned hand-painted crockery,
though fast dying out, is still occasionally made.

I enjoyed greatly this last summer watching the growth of a tame teasel which was
sown from some seed swept by the maid out
of the drawing-room, where we had some

Teasel.

teasel heads in a vase. The first year the
plant did nothing but lay its foundations,
spreading out a star of hard green leaves,
closely pressed to the ground, as though
claiming the portion of room it required for

M

the development of its future superstructure ;
but this spring it began to shoot up, and
flourished amazingly, delighting every one by
its vigorous growth, stately habit, and sym-
metrical arrangement.   This plant is fond of
water, as its name, " Dipsacus," indicates, and

Section of Water-cups of the Teasel.

in its growth has an ingenious method of
supplying itself as it mounts up higher and
higher: each pair of leaves are united at their
bases and form a sort of cup, as shown in my
diagram ; in this quite a quantity of water is
retained—water which either comes from the
rain, or in dry weather from the dew running

down from the leaves. Small flies, etc.,
get drowned in these receptacles, but I do
not know whether the plant is of a carnivorous character and derives any benefit from
their carcases. The backs of the leaves of

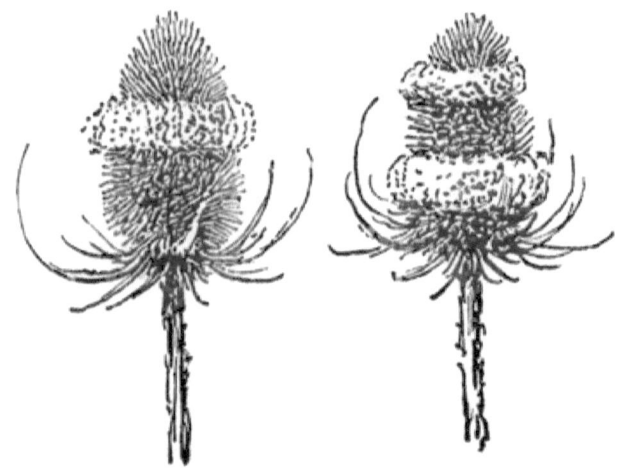

First and Second Stage of Bloom of Teasel.

the teasel have small, recurved, hook-like
spines up the rib, which, in a state of nature,
serve to moor the tall plant amongst its
surroundings.

You know, no doubt, the shape of the
teasel head, but perhaps were not aware that
the centre and largest head is not the tallest ;

it opens in bloom first, but is always over-
topped by its side shoots.   The bloom comes
out in a ring round the centre at first, and
then parts into an upper and lower ring in a
picturesque way.   When in bloom, the bees
are never away from it.   I send you a little
sketch of the teasel.

G. D. L.

LETTER XXV

23rd November 1889.

DEAR MARCO—On my return from town yesterday I saw two instances of the disregard that birds pay to the passing of trains. Between Moulsford and Wallingford I saw a kingfisher perched on a small rail over a brook which ran under the line, scarcely a foot or two from the base of the low embankment, and it remained perfectly unmoved whilst the train passed. I saw also a kestrel-hawk, almost immediately afterwards, flying along low to the ground, so close to the edge of the embankment that I could plainly see the beautiful brown and barred marks on the back and wings as I looked down on it;

the fact that the bird flew along the way the
train was going giving me quite an excep-
tionally good opportunity of observing it.
In a former letter I spoke of the birds I saw
from the train whilst going from Reading to
Marlborough ; and whenever I have done
that journey since, the tameness of birds as
regards the passing trains has struck me as
very remarkable ; so near an approach to
any of these birds on foot would have been
simply impossible.

Instinct as to danger seems very strongly
implanted in the brute animals. I remember
seeing bullocks resisting to their utmost to
pass up a narrow passage leading to a
slaughter - house which they could never
have seen in their life before, and after some
trouble enticed in by means of a horse,
which was led up the passage, the bullocks
following from the confidence they had in
their fellow-creature. It is said that it is
the smell of blood that excites the animal's
suspicions ; but the horse pays no attention

to this, having grown accustomed to it by habit.

The only other thing I had noted down to write to you about, was as to the variety of ways the climbing plants have of attaching and supporting their growth. The tendrils of the pea family with their curiously hooked ends, the grappling hooks and the sucker-like attachments of the ampelopsis, the clinging tendrils of the ivy, and the twisting grip of the bindweeds are all well known. The clematis, tomato, and some others form kinks in their leaf-stems, which secure the plants very effectively. Thorns are the great supporters to the rose family. A wild rose or a bramble is very securely moored in a hedge by means of its hooked thorns; and as no plants like less to be blown about, this close mooring is very important to them. I spoke in my last of the hooks at the back of the teasel leaves, which steady the young growth most effectually. I believe a great amount of support is afforded to slender shoots by the many cobwebs and lines of the spiders to which I alluded in a former letter. The troublesome weeds called "cleavers" sustain themselves by the minute hooks that cover their stems and seeds—these latter often get into the fur of dogs and cats, to their very great discomfort.

G. D. L.

11th January 1892.

DEAR MARCO—The gap in my correspondence is very lamentable ; perhaps the less that is said about it the better.

Beyond the remarkable frost that occurred last winter (1890-91), there is nothing extremely out of the way to recount ; this frost was, however, quite an event, beginning in the latter part of November and continuing until nearly the end of January.

During the last three weeks of this period the river was frozen over from bank to bank, forming a regular highway for skaters. With a few breaks here and there, people could

skate from Oxford to Reading. This frost
happened most luckily during the Christmas
holidays, so that my boys got the full benefit
of it, skating nearly from morning to night.
I have not skated myself since I have been
married; as you, I daresay, remember. I had
a nasty fall on the ice a short time before
that event, which laid me on my back for
three weeks; but I brought out my tricycle
and had some delightful runs on the ice,
being able to go many miles. The ice at
the sides of the river grew enormously thick;
every now and then, as the river rose or fell,
cracks opened along the banks and the surface would get flooded; as of course this
froze, the ice thickened above and below at
the same time—in places the ice must have
been considerably over a foot in thickness.
At intervals of about twenty yards there were
large cracks which extended right across the
river; a little water would ooze up through
these when they first occurred, and then
they froze again harder than ever; they

were occasioned by the rise and fall of the river. At Abingdon a cart and horse were driven along on the ice, and a sheep roasted; both which experiments might have been carried out safely at Wallingford. At Benson Weir and Lock icicles were formed of huge size and of the most grotesque appearance.

I am sorry to say that this long frost killed vast quantities of birds of all sorts; a diminishment in their numbers being distinctly noticeable last year. Kingfishers were especially hard put to it. The only open water to be found was where some springs or little brooks ran into the river, such as those at Ewelme, Mongewell, or North Stoke; but even here fish were very scarce. I need not say that we put food for the birds every day in our garden; numbers of all sorts came daily for their dole; even the moor-hens grew very tame, feeding like ordinary poultry.

The frost was never very severe in in-

tensity, its long continuance being its chief
peculiarity ; there were now and then slight
thaws, but never of length sufficient to break
up the ice in any way. The sight from our
house was most curious, the river being
turned into a regular highroad.

The final thaw began on 20th January, but
it took nearly a week to break up the ice on
the river entirely. The ice in front of our
house gave way in a remarkable manner.
At about 8.30 on the morning of the 24th
January, as I was dressing, on looking out
from my bedroom window I suddenly became
aware that the whole surface of ice was
moving in one mass down stream. It had no
doubt given way below somewhere, and crack-
ing off from the edges of the banks simul-
taneously, the vast sheet of ice moved off *en
masse ;* in a very few minutes the whole was
gone, and there was the river again running
as we had not seen it doing for more than a
month. Wallingford Bridge of course kept
back the ice above for a short time longer,

the ice floating down gradually in large
pieces. The jagged edges of solid ice along
the banks remained for a long time; much
damage being here and there done when the
floods came and carried them off, tearing up
many willows and bushes to which they
were frozen.

I have during the last year added to my
live stock, now having a duck and drake and
two pigs. The ducks are perhaps purely
ornamental, as I cannot succeed in rearing
any young ones; but they have amused me
greatly. The first duck died soon after I
had her, leaving the drake disconsolate; but
at last he consoled himself by forming a firm
attachment to my donkey, "Rosie"; following her about wherever she went continually,
sleeping beside her in the stable, feeding
close to her nose, lying down when she lay
down, getting up when she got up; when
Rosie brayed the drake flapped his wings and
quacked. It was most curious, and showed
what craving there is for fellowship amongst

the brute creation. One of my lady friends, hearing of this drake's bereavement, presented me with a beautiful young duck, which was duly introduced to the old drake. Then a

Rosie and the Drake.

curious scene took place; the drake at once left Rosie and ran to meet the duck with the greatest delight and eagerness, standing by her with fondness and affection. I must here say that this drake was very dirty in his habits, never using a little pond I had made for him or washing in any way much; whereas the duck had come from a place where cleanliness was the rule, she having a nice pond in which to swim. The duck, then, after her journey in the hamper, feeling no doubt rather frowsy, and seeing the little pond, at once launched herself on it, and began her ablutions most energetically. The old drake seemed terribly alarmed, running round the edge of the pond and doing all he could to get the duck to come out, until finding she took no notice of his entreaties he finally left her to herself, and ran off in the most unmistakable pique to rejoin his old love Rosie again. Since then he has grown more accustomed to his wife's ways, and even in the summer-time takes a tub himself occasionally.

This little episode of the drake and Rosie reminded me of Titania's love for Bottom; only in this case the sexes were reversed.

The pigs I buy young and fatten up and sell. They are of a good sort, called here

" Blue Berkshire."   There is always a profit on pigs, it seems to me, when there is much refuse food for them from the house.

I have also bought a pony for Peter to learn to ride on ; he gets on better than I expected with his riding, and, as the pony is a very quiet one, seldom falls off.   Influenza is very rampant down here ; we have had it more or less, but are all well at present again.   I am struggling with, what for me is, quite a large picture ; but the cold weather is trying, as I cannot keep my fingers warm enough for work for any length of time.

G. D. L.

1st February 1892.

DEAR MARCO—You seemed amused by my account of the loves of Rosie and the drake, so perhaps you would like to hear a little more about Rosie. I know not her exact age, but she was given to me some eight years ago by my friend Madame Maës of West Quay, Southampton, who purchased her from some gipsies when quite a foal. At West Quay all animals are treated as friends and relations, so Rosie was brought up in a very indulged manner, being made a great pet of by Madame M. and her daughters.

N

These latter would sometimes dress her up in
their hats and shawls, and even take her
indoors, teaching her to drink coffee from a
cup, neatly, with her lips, as a human being
would : an art which she has never lost.   I
now in cold weather always give her some
breakfast thus ; she never spills any, or at-
tempts to bite the cup in any way.   When
she left West Quay for Wallingford she gave
great trouble at the railway station.   I was
told that she had thirteen porters round her,
and objected so strongly to enter the horse-
box that at last she had to be lifted bodily in.
At the other end of her journey she came out
quite quietly, and very soon made herself at
home here.   She has been most useful and
interesting to me since I have had her ; she
works the mowing-machine and takes the
children out in a little cart.   Donkeys are
extremely clever animals, and I never could
understand why stupid people should have
been called after them.   They are most dainty
feeders, and in a meadow with cows and

horses always lead the browsing, the other
animals seeming to respect their superior
judgment as to the choice of feeding-ground.
That donkeys eat and enjoy thistles is also,
as far as I have been able to find out, a gross
fiction. Of course they appreciate the sow-
thistle as do any other animals, but the
common prickly thistle Rosie refuses to
touch on any consideration ; I have tried
her over and over again. In these parts the
donkey is truly the poor man's friend, the
amount done by their help and a small cart
being astonishing.

Up at Ipsden and Nuffield are several
deep wells in the chalk, which are worked by
large wooden wheels, inside of which donkeys
go, like a squirrel in his revolving cage. One
such is at Ipsden House, where Charles
Reade was born, and where his ancestors
resided for years. I believe there is such an
one at Carisbrooke Castle, though I have never
seen it. These wheels are extremely picturesque, with their surrounding wood-work, and

one of them would make a good subject for
your pencil.

On one occasion when Rosie had taken
some of my children in the cart to a small
picnic, she was placed in a sort of stable at
an inn on account of the rain.   Here she
found a large corn-bin, the lid of which she
is supposed to have lifted ; at any rate, she
was found right inside the bin when they
came for her ; how she managed it I do not
know.

I am sorry to say since my last letter
Rosie has been a victim to the influenza, both
she and the pony having suffered from it ;
both are coming round very satisfactorily,
and I have no anxiety about them.

I paid a visit, one day in September last,
to a very old farm-house at South Moreton,
not far from here, which would have greatly
delighted you.   The house was of all periods
as to its construction, having parts quite as
old as the Tudors.   One wing, the oldest,
had been disused for living in for many years,

but the good old oak beams and strong work generally had resisted the effects of time. In the old kitchen was a hen with a large brood of chickens, which were on quite friendly terms with a cat and her kittens, the kitties played with the chickens harmlessly.

Above the kitchen, up a very small and twisted staircase, were some quaint old rooms, used now as apple-lofts and lumber-rooms. In one was an old door which opened right into the huge chimney from the kitchen below; in this chimney were numbers of hooks and bars on which bacon used to be hung and placed for the purpose of smoking.

The farmer, a very old man, showed me an old rate-book of the last century,—church rates I think this book contained,—and it was surprising to find column after column filled with expenditure accounts for such items as these :

To so-and-so for one dozen sparheads .	3d.
To so-and-so for a pole-cat . .	6d.
To so-and-so for one hedgehock .	4d.

quite large sums being spent annually in the destruction of sparrows and other so-considered vermin. These books were all signed by the churchwardens for the time being. These old rate-books are always worth looking into, as they throw great light on the doings of olden times.

Wallingford has been going through a period of upheaval on account of drainage works, the whole borough having had to abolish the old drains and adopt a new system called "the Shone," which is to carry the sewage away from the river and up to a sewage-farm in the fields at the west of the town.

I expected in such a very old town as this many interesting things would have turned up during the excavations, but this has not been the case ; beyond one or two skeletons and bones in general, little has been found. I secured a curious old horse-shoe, which, with some horses' bones, was dug up near here from a depth of eight feet ; the bones were very black and hard, the shoe flat and broad, the iron being very thin, but of fine quality, ringing like a bell when struck.　It is of this shape, and has not the little turned-up bit in front which modern shoes have.

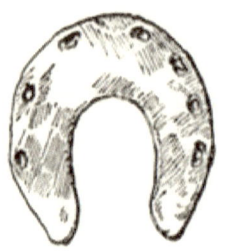

Old Horse-shoe.

I believe a few coins were found ; but these were all taken to a Mr. Davis,[1] who lives here, who has a very large and valuable collection of coins and other antiquities.　Any coins that are found in this neighbourhood by workmen are generally taken to him, as he always gives a fair price for them.　Mr. Davis has one cabinet of coins which he told me he insured for £6000.　He is courteous and obliging, and very pleased to show his treasures to those who ask to see them at any time.

He is very well known to the people at the British Museum, and is well up in numis-matics.　He has amassed a prodigious quantity

---

[1] Mr. Davis has, I am sorry to say, died since this was written.

of flint arrow-heads and other implements,
which are found in numbers on the hills

Flint from which an Arrow-head has been struck off.

around here.   Mr. Davis has also repeatedly
found flints from which arrow-heads have

been cut off, like the one in my
sketch.   Mr. Davis goes to
look for these things in the
newly ploughed fields after any
heavy rain-storms, as the most
likely time to discover them.

Arrow-head.

He has a very quick eye for detecting

Flint knife.

them.   Some he has are most beautifully
shaped, like this; and he has a flint knife

which is still quite sharp, of this shape. How those primeval fellows managed to make these weapons by simply chipping, I own quite passes my comprehension. Mr. Davis's other antiquities, though curious, are very mixed in character.

I cannot tell you how much I would give for a visit from you just now, even for a day, just to consult over my struggles with my picture. I am more and more impressed how great is the value of friendly communion amongst brother artists, now that I am so debarred from it, and one morning's visit from my old trusted Marco would be indeed a pleasure and a profit to me.

G. D. L.

LETTER XXVIII

22nd February 1892.

DEAR MARCO—In the autumn of 1890
we saw a good deal of the cavalry manœuvres
which took place on the downs near here.
Amongst other things, the soldiers were to
practise fording the river on horseback. We
went down on several days to Little Stoke
Ferry to see this operation, which was rather
a failure, as only a few men and one or two
officers went across on one day, and even
that we missed seeing; but I saw a young
farmer cross the river several times mounted
on a gray horse. He rode his horse down to
the river; the animal walked deliberately in,

and when it became too deep, giving a plunge forward, at the same time making a sort of blowing noise, swam over quite easily. When the swimming began, the man, slipping off on one side, struck out with his legs, holding on to the horse by the mane. The horse did not seem to mind it in the least, and when the other bank was reached, the man, who had remounted on reaching shallow water, turned the horse round, and recrossed the river in the same way.

Last year I saw a cow that was in a meadow opposite our house swim the river. The cow had been separated from its companions, and was exceedingly restless, pacing up and down the bank and lowing continually. It saw my neighbour's cows on the other side, and evidently wished much to join them; at last she took deliberately to the water, walking quietly in and swimming across with the greatest ease. She looked like a small boat in the water, as the top part of her back showed its whole length. I was

much astonished, the more so as the river
was in partial flood at the time, by the good
progress she made. When the other bank
was reached, my neighbour's cows refused
to let her land, so she floundered along by
the edge of the river, and finally went up
through the bridge and landed on the tow-
path above it.

The sight of this cow's swimming helped
me to the better understanding of one of
Bewick's little vignettes. If you turn to your
second volume of *The British Birds*, p. 173,
and look at the tailpiece to the chapter on
the little auk, you will find the one to which
I refer. It represents a niggardly man
crossing a river with his cow, which he holds
by the tail; he is using the ford to escape
the payment of the toll of the bridge, which
is seen behind; there is a waggon crossing
and a man on horseback stopping to pay at
the little toll-house. The stingy man has
already lost his hat; and his nose, small as
the cut is, looks nipt and cold; whilst, to

add to his miseries, it is winter, snow being
on the distant hills, the river is in flood, and
two boys are sliding on the ice at the edge
of the river on the farther side.   I always
used to think this man would either be
drowned or have to abandon the cow; but I

Vignette from Bewick.

believe now he is meant to be intending to
cross with the cow, that she will tow him
safely across if he holds on, and that the man
has been in the habit of doing it to save the
toll.

À propos of Bewick, have you ever noticed
what an immense number of his tailpieces

refer to crossing rivers?—men on stilts, in boats, on stepping-stones, on the ice, etc. There is a black cat crossing on a plank too, and very many bridges of one sort and another.

Cats are generally considered to be extremely averse to going into the water, but I have seen river-side cats at times swim very well. We have a young jet-black tom-cat named Chibo, which is constantly down by the edge of the river, especially when Peter is fishing, and which often gets into the water; it is true, generally by accident. It will also go out in the punt with Peter of its own accord. One day one of my boys climbed from off an overhanging willow into a large dredging-punt which was moored a considerable distance from the bank, and Chibo followed him into the boat; my son came ashore by the tree, but Chibo deliberately walked up to the end of the punt, and, taking a header, swam ashore quite easily, his tail stretched out like a rudder behind him. Whenever Chibo gets

wet like this he runs straight into the kitchen
to be wiped and dried.   He is a very great
favourite of the cook.

The late cold weather has kept the plants
in my garden in very backward condition,
though the ground is alive with little nubs
and noses of all sorts poking through, and
ready to start on the least accession of heat.
These early-flowering plants have different
sorts of protection afforded them from the cold
they have to face.   I mentioned the Pasque
flower, *Anemone pulsatilla*, in a former letter;
it blooms about Easter-time generally,
whence its name.   On the bleak chalk downs
around here it is often found.   In its wild
state it grows very dwarf, and its first buds
are enveloped in a thick woolly coat, but in
a garden with shelter it develops considerably; when wild it throws up but one solitary
flower, but under cultivation numbers of
blooms arise with far longer stalks.   After
the bloom is over, it sends out a quantity of
foliage which has no wool about it.   This

plant, however, often dies away under cultivation in a garden, becoming enervated and
exhausted in some way after a bit.

You know that all animals assume some
sort of change in their clothing as winter
approaches, casting it off again when summer
returns.   I heard of rather a curious circum-
stance as to this from a gentleman at Newbury, who told me he had had a present of a
horse and a dog sent him from Australia.
They arrived in England in the middle of our
summer, and both had on their winter coats,
which they had just put on when they left
Australia.   The horse very soon shed his
coat, and as winter came on grew another;
but the poor dog never shed his until his
usual time in November, in consequence
of which he took cold and died in the
winter.

My seedling teasels are quite curious in
their manner of sturdy growth.   Just now
they are apparently at rest, but the tight hold
they keep of the patches of soil they require

is very remarkable ; nothing can get beneath these flat, strong, green stars. No doubt they are laying the foundations for the " Eiffel Towers " that are to shoot up in the coming summer.

G. D. L.

LETTER XXIX

13th April 1892.

DEAR MARCO — After ten days of very
warm cloudless weather, the winter temperature returned yesterday, and now it is snowing
and raining with a cruel north-east wind.   It
is not quite so bad as was the return of the
cold last year, which occurred later on and did
great damage.   This year the long spell of
dry north-east winds has retarded the growth
of most things, so that there is little above
ground to hurt ; and, as rain of any sort was
much wanted, I am more hopeful.

Last year the return of winter took place
after the swallows had arrived, and the mor-

tality amongst them was truly pitiable. In
my boat-house any quantity of swallows and
martins collected to roost at night. They
huddled together in one long row, like my
sketch, on an iron bar near the roof,[1] and
every morning I used to pick up three or four
dead ones that must have perished during the

Swallows at roost.

night. As the weather grew better, they
gave up this night-refuge and disappeared;
but it was remarkable, no swallows built new,
or used the old nests that summer in the
boat-house; indeed there were very few about
this place at all last year.

My Pasque flowers are out and very fine
this year, and I enclose one for Agnes.

[1] I believe this cold iron bar was bad for the swallows, and
was the cause of so many falling dead from it during the nights.
I have put a small wooden bar up now, and the swallows much
prefer it.

They must be brave-hearted plants to stand
the cold on the downs as they do, thriving
there and spreading on the northern sides of
the slopes in large colonies. On these downs
you will find, too, a golden thistle, a mere

Anemone pulsatilla, the " Pasque Flower."

prickly star with no stalk at all, which defies
the wind and cold. The cultivated tulip of
our gardens fares badly in rain and snow, as
its early flowering and large upturned bloom
does not shut nearly so tight in the cold as a
crocus does. Its thick stalk is rigid, and gives
no protection by bending over. The less

cultivated species of tulips, such as the Gesner,
have longer stems, which bend, and thus help
the bloom to throw off the rain, and the little
wild tulip droops like a fritillary.   Large
masses of this wild tulip are found in a cover
in a park at Chiselhampton, about eight miles
from here, where also a curious species of
martagon lily has become naturalised in a
very remarkable manner.

In the spring the old man's fancy lightly
turns to thoughts of flowers, as this letter
seems to show; so I may as well here mention
that, fond as I am of wild flowers, and much
as I have lived in the country, it was not
until a year ago that I ever saw two rather
rare plants growing.   One, the deadly nightshade, *Atropa belladonna*, which I recog-
nised in a moment by its large black fruit,
unlike anything I had ever seen, each berry
by itself growing at the base of each pair
of leaves all the way up the stem.   In
the woods where I saw it first it was
a handsome shrub, and grew gracefully

beneath the protection of tall beech trees on
a steep chalky bank ; but I have since seen it
growing at Ipsden on a rabbit-warren, quite
in the open, where it was of a far more ragged
character in growth. The flower is rather
insignificant, and has a vicious and uncanny
look. The rabbits evidently carefully avoided
it. It is not a common plant, nor nearly
so beautiful as the woody nightshade, but
it is deadly poisonous, and is the plant
from which belladonna is derived. The
old-fashioned name of the plant is dwale,
probably derived from *deuil*, the French for
mourning.

The other plant, which I had never seen,
is one which is not found at all in this
neighbourhood, and yet I saw it here by a
curious chance twice on the same day. Last
year Alma Tadema was at Streatley for a
short time during the summer. I went over
to see him one afternoon, and found Mrs.
Tadema sitting in the garden, and by her
side a pot containing a little plant which I at

once knew, from my book-knowledge, must
be one called the Grass of Parnassus. It is
a very pretty and rather uncommon bog-
plant. Mrs. Tadema had had it given to
her, and she had carried it to Streatley
with her.

But it was curious that on the same afternoon I should have seen another specimen.
I called on a lady to whom I had given some
Japanese irises, to see how they were getting
on ; and there, round the base of these irises,
were one or two little plants of this same
Parnassia. The lady was of Norfolk extraction, and knew the plant well as a girl ; but it
was puzzling to think how it had found its way
to her garden in Oxfordshire. We accounted
for it in this way. I had advised her that
these irises required plenty of moisture and
a peaty soil, and she had planted them near
a large pond, and put some lumps of peat into
the ground, and no doubt the little seeds or
roots of the Parnassia came there in the peat,
possibly even from Norfolk.

I am making a small bog garden here, and hope next year to have this pretty little plant growing in it, along with sundew, buck bean, water violets, butterwort, and other hardy bog-plants.

G. D. L.

LETTER XXX

4th May 1892.

DEAR MARCO—No doubt you have read
the two lectures by Professor Ruskin, which
he entitles " The Storm-cloud of the Nine-
teenth Century."   In them is described, in the
most wonderfully accurate manner, that sort of
blight of bad weather which seems to have
fallen upon us in these latter days.   His description of what he calls the plague or devil
wind is singularly correct; its character,
persistence, and effects being dwelt on with
that marvellous power of language for which
he is so famous.   One thing which he points
out as characteristic of this wind is that its

baneful nature does not seem to be influenced by the quarter from whence it blows. Most of us can remember when an east wind was dry and cold, a south wind warm and wet, a west wind bright and clear, and a north wind bright and cold, but now we seem to have dark, cold winds, persistently recurring from all quarters alike. The Professor allows that there are intervals of fine and even lovely weather, but the phenomenon is in the ever-returning spells of this plague wind. A few years ago this wind was of a damp and rainy character, but certainly during this year and the last it has been one of cold and drought.[1] In all years it has been attended with darkness and gloom; the clouds being, as he

---

[1] The drought which has again prevailed this present spring, for even a longer period than it did last year, has, according to my observations, been attended by the same cold north-east wind; though this has been much tempered by the extraordinary amount of bright sunshine. Amongst other curious results of the prevalence of bright sunshine this year, the tulip tree has bloomed freely in England : a friend of mine yesterday gave me a beautiful specimen of the flower from a tree in Hertfordshire. I never saw it in England but once before, about forty years ago, on a tree in Cashiobury Park.—*17th June* 1893.

describes them, of paltry shapelessness. I
have been noting in my diary for the last two
years the state of the weather, and find that
the wind in question has been blowing with
its curiously pertinacious character almost
entirely from the north and north-east. Even
when, in the winter, we had the wind from
the south it was not accompanied by warmth
or rain, some of the severest frosts having
taken place when the wind was south. I have
waited in vain for any explanations, or even
recognition, from the meteorological experts
of this singular state of affairs. These gentlemen would, of course, pay little attention to
Mr. Ruskin's lectures, regarding them, no
doubt, as unworthy of any serious scientific
consideration ; but for all that I am convinced,
from my own experiences, the Professor never
wrote anything that was more true in fact and
description.

To-day and yesterday the character of the
wind has been remarkably baneful, and these
two days might be taken as good types of the

prevailing weather for the last two years.
Though these cold north winds have occasionally been accompanied by rain or drizzel, as
they are to-day, the two years have been ones
of drought, so that now, in spite of the heavy
but short downpour and flood which took
place last October, the river is very low, and
the people on the hills are again short of
water, as they were all last summer and
autumn.

It is not inspiriting weather, and my
garden has little of interest in it, even if it
were not so cold. I planted a few annuals
and some new perennials, amongst which is
one called *Dictamnus fraxinella*, in English
" Burning Bush." This is rather a pretty
plant, the bloom of which emits, at certain
seasons, a sort of gas which ignites when a
flame is put to it. I had never seen this
plant until now, and you may imagine how
anxiously I shall await the trial of its peculiarity.

I have made great havoc amongst the

snails and slugs. One or two warm days last week brought out a large batch of hibernating tabbies which went at once, no doubt by scent instinct, to my iris clumps, where I found them just before they had commenced to break their long fast. I have seen none since, the dry cold having most likely stopped them back. Small snails and slugs do not seem to mind the cold, and I slaughter hundreds. The snails and slugs must have a strong instinct of scent; as I found, when my boys placed sugar and beer on the trees to collect night-moths, very many large slugs greedily feeding on the bait.

I also found, whenever I have left the mangled remains of a slug or snail on a low brick wall, that two or more slugs in a very short time would be attracted by the scent and proceed to feed greedily on their dead companion. So, to his other disagreeable qualities, the slug must have added the crime of cannibalism. I in this way kill slugs at a sort of compound interest. It reminds one of people catching their deaths by attending funerals. Excuse a rather gloomy and depressing letter, dear Marco; I promise to cheer up the moment the weather brightens again.

G. D. L.

LETTER XXXI

6th May 1892.

DEAR MARCO—The sight of the sun this morning and the receipt of your letter with the charming book-plate revived me greatly from my despondency. The sun certainly shines to-day, though the wind is still fierce and cold from the north. The book-plate is, however, an unmixed pleasure, and I look forward to the delight of sticking it in all my most valued book treasures, eagerly. Many, many thanks, dear Marco, for the pains and skill you have bestowed upon it. Grieved am I to hear of your rheumatic attack, and trust it may soon pass away. My wife, who is subject to rheumatism, invariably finds the

GEORGE·D·LESLIE·

Book-plate designed by H. S. Marks, R.A., for the Author.

north-east winds are those which bring on
the attacks.   This connection between the
complaint and the north-east wind is most remarkable, and renders its prevailing persist-
ency all the more deplorable.   I daresay you
remember this wind and how we suffered
from it when we visited Pulborough ; how
cold and colourless everything looked under
its influence.   We had been always so
accustomed to fine weather on our former
sketching excursions, that the contrast was
all the more striking.   I recollect that it cul-
minated in a snow-storm, during which the
race for the Derby was run and won by
Hermit.

I think that was the first time I had ever
noticed the want of colour that accompanies
a north-east wind ; sky, trees, and grass all
looking washed out and drabby.   I have been
particularly struck with this colourless aspect
lately ; there is always a white haze or glare
round the sun, which seems to bleach its rays,
and when a few thin beggarly clouds pass

P

over, it appears, as the Professor so happily expresses it, exactly "like a bad half-crown at the bottom of a basin of soap-suds."

I hope you will have a pleasant dinner[1] to-morrow, and wish I was to be present, so as to hear your little speech.

G. D. L.

---

[1] The Artists' General Benevolent Fund Dinner, at which Mr. Marks returned thanks for The Royal Society of Water-Colour Painters.

LETTER XXXII

13th May 1892.

Dear Marco—Though the chill north
wind continues to blow, the sun has shone
every day during the last week. The land
is suffering dreadfully for want of rain ; trees,
shrubs, grass, etc., making hardly any progress ; but the temperature of the water in the
river has greatly increased under the pro-
longed sunshine, and swarms of little fish of
all sorts abound.

Now little fish on tender stone
Begin to cast their bellies,
And sluggish snails, that erst were mewed,
Do creep out of their shellies ;

The rumbling rivers now do warm,
For little boys to paddle ;
The sturdy steed now goes to grass,
And up they hang his saddle.
                    BEAUMONT AND FLETCHER.

I now enjoy much sitting on the steps of
our landing-stage, in the warm sun, watching
the small bleak, chub, roach, etc.   The little
bleak are rotund with spawn ; at least they
were so last Sunday, the 8th ; but some fish
must have spawned much earlier, as I noticed
shoals of minute fry.   Fish swim by almost
the exactly opposite method to that by which
a bird flies.   Birds propel themselves with
their wings and steer with their tails, whereas
fish propel themselves with their tails and
steer with their fins or wings.

The dart forward is accomplished entirely
by the action of the fish's tail, the pectoral
fins being tightly closed to the sides.   These
pectoral fins are principally used for backing
or stopping.   The bird's tail, as I formerly
mentioned, serves as a very powerful brake

THE LANDING-STAGE, RIVERSIDE.

to arrest the speed, though it cannot be used
for backing, as the pectoral fins of the fish.

In my sketch of a jack you will notice how
very large the dorsal and anal fins are.   They
are set far back, close to the tail, and, taken
together, form almost a second large tail.   I
have no doubt they give an enormous assist-
ance to the propelling power, making the rush

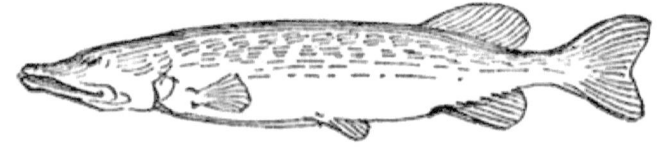

Sketch of a Jack.

forward extremely rapid.   In most fishes
these two fins serve chiefly as keels to steady
the fish.   The pectoral and centre fins no
doubt do the steering.   All these fins can be
closed or expanded at will.

A pair of swans have this year taken up
their quarters in front of our house.   They
are young birds, probably driven away from
their birthplace by their parents.   They are
very much in love with one another at

present, and their ways are very pretty to
watch.   Birds are not, I believe, much given
to kissing, though we hear of "billing and
cooing." I think I have seen doves taking
each other's bills, one in another ; at any rate
these swans may be said to kiss, for they
cross and clasp each other's bills very prettily,
and rub and fondle their heads and necks
together.   The tom is very gallant in defence
of his mate, surging round her at the approach of any boat or person on the bank.
He acted, too, in a way I remember my
game-cock used to do, as a sort of encour-
agement to a hen to take to the nest.   The
cock would often get into the nest and turn
round and round in it, calling the hen all
the time.   The tom-swan, in like manner,
landed on a likely spot amongst some rushes,
and commenced plucking dry reeds, sticks,
etc., which he threw over his back and
trampled down, evidently nest-building.   The
hen meanwhile kept close by, swimming round
and round and making a sort of moaning purr,

which noise I imagine was analogous to the grating sound a hen makes when she contemplates laying an egg.

I was spending a few days, a short time ago, at a friend's house near Newbury, and heard a very well authenticated story about some owls. A gentleman who had a number of pigeons in a regular cote, having noticed a great falling off in the number of the birds, made search into the interior, and there discovered, at home with the pigeons, a pair of old owls, a pair of young owls, and a pair of nestling owls; these latter had their suppers laid out before them in the most orderly manner, consisting of a pair of half-fledged squabs. I am sorry to have to relate this story, as I am so fond of owls, having believed hitherto that they fed chiefly on mice and beetles; but no doubt these birds having found the dove-cot a convenient roosting-place, innocently took up their abode in it, giving way gradually to the temptation as their families increased.

Mr. Fisher, at whose house I was staying, possesses an old family picture : a hunting piece, with portraits of two of his ancestors, hare-hunting. I have made a little outline

William and Richard Fisher, Esq., hunting at Park Place, Henley.

of part of this picture for you. One of the squires has a buff-coloured coat and the other a blue one ; both have scarlet waistcoats and cocked hats. The old house is Park Place, Henley. There is a parson who has come to grief on the ground behind.

In the other part of the picture, which I have
not drawn, are the huntsmen and hounds,
with a view of Marsh Weir and the river in
the distance.   Mr. Richard Fisher, the celebrated collector of old woodcuts and engrav-
ings, was a descendant of one of these old
squires; as was also, I believe, John Con-
stable's friend Archdeacon Fisher.   The
date of this picture is 1709.   These two
gentlemen were jolly old hunting squires;
and on one occasion they had a drag drawn
through Henley Town, and the hounds set
on the scent at twelve o'clock at night,
the whole hunt, with horns, etc., rushing
through the streets in the moonlight, causing great amazement amongst the sleeping
townspeople.   From the look of their jolly
faces in the picture, I should say they were
just the men to have enjoyed doing this.
They are buried in Hambleden churchyard,
and Mr. Fisher has a cane and snuff-box
which belonged to one of them.

G. D. L.

Extracts from two Letters from Marco to G. D. L.

I

17th May 1892.

As to the kissing of birds, I noticed when we kept doves—*Turtur risorius*, with the little black ring round its neck—they were always doing one of three things : eating, fighting, or love-making ; and when engaged in the latter occupation, would tenderly kiss with intertwined bills for several minutes at a time.

At the Zoo, not only the love-birds, who are extremely fond, will kiss and caress each other, but the cockatoos, including the larger

sulphur-crested ones and the parrakeets. Of
the macaws I have no opportunities of knowing, as these birds are,--why, I don't know,--
always kept on single stands and never placed
in pairs. One pair of moderate-sized white
cockatoos appear to be a very devoted couple ;
they are nearly always close to one another,
and not only does the " billing " go on very
warmly, but the male will caress with his bill
the head and neck of the female, while she
half closes her eyes in quiet satisfaction and
enjoyment.

I saw Mr. Tegetmeier yesterday, and had
some interesting chat with him. Among other
things, he said people make a mistake in
baiting a trap for rats. You may catch a
young, but never an old one with it. He
says, place a piece of board against the wall
of a run or place infested with them ; the rat
will always in his run go between the wall
and the board, and here is your opportunity.
Place a gin-trap, a small one, unbaited (he
gets his at 4s. the dozen), between the

board and the wall, with a little soft loose straw over it, and the rat will, in passing through the aperture, be caught by the leg.

Of birds, he said, only two were enemies to the agriculturist (not the horticulturist): the sparrow, whom he called the parasite of man, and the rook.   At one time, for a whole year, he had a hundred sparrows sent him once a month ; he opened all their crops, but never discovered anything but corn or grains. Young sparrows will take insects from the parent bird, but when they come to maturity they prefer a vegetable diet.   Rooks, he said, will take corn in very dry weather, when the ground is too hard for the easy procuring of grubs.

Many other things of interest he told me, but he talked so rapidly that I am afraid I might mar a curious tale in telling it. . . .

H. S. M.

II

23rd May 1892.

MY DEAR GEORGE—I have just returned from an hour at the Zoo, where I have had a talk with Mr. Bartlett, the superintendent. As regards the " kissing " of birds, he says many birds do clasp their bills together, and it is no doubt a form of caressing prior to love-making; but as to calling it " kissing," he says that is but a sentimental way of looking at it. The Chinaman does not kiss his wife, but licks her face as a cat does that of her kittens; with doves and pigeons the act of " kissing " is to propel half digested food into each other's mouths, in the same way as they feed their young.

Birds of the hawk tribe, and even the lordly eagle, will, when in a loving mood, go through the process of "billing" with their mates. Bartlett, to whom I read that part of your letter relating to swans and owls, said it was no uncommon thing for the latter to make themselves at home in pigeon-houses if they can manage it without interference; and they will eat the eggs and young of other birds if they get the chance. He corroborated what Tegetmeier said about the sparrows and the rooks. Rooks are great nuisances to them at the Zoo; he says they will steal the food provided for the birds, and eat the eggs and the young of the inmates if they get the opportunity. On one occasion he assured me a rook made off with a *swan's egg*, which, as you know, is of considerable size. He managed this by inserting his bill into the egg, in which was a cygnet almost ready to be hatched. Some part of the unfortunate creature's body gave him a hold, and he carried it about two hundred yards; but the weight proving too heavy for him, he dropped it by the western aviary and made off unencumbered.

Bartlett is a man who would interest you very much ; not only is he a keen observer, but he has travelled much in his time. Last year the Society sent him out to the Canary Islands, so as to enable him to avoid the rigour of that terrible winter and establish his health. Physically, he is a wonderful man between seventy and eighty, very wiry, and full of energy and go.

H. S. M.

LETTER XXXIII

24th May 1892.

DEAR MARCO — Your two letters with
notes on the "billing" habits of birds are
most interesting. Mr. Tegetmeier and Mr.
Bartlett are real authorities, and I envy you
much the pleasure of their acquaintance.
My untutored observations on nature can
of course bear no sort of comparison, in point
of value, with the experiences of such men
as these ; but I am an artist and trained to see
things ; I have, too, a deep love of nature, and
no doubt on this account, as well as for old
friendship's sake, my letters are acceptable to
you. Mr. Bartlett seems to think my term

kissing, as applied to the actions of the swans, rather a sentimental one ; but I do not see this : it is only the difference between lips and bills ; the intention and satisfaction of the process is the same, and equally promoted, in either the case of man or bird, by feelings of mutual love.   I, for my own part, am not ashamed of being sentimental.   I think "the one touch of nature that makes the whole world kin" would not be much of a touch or help towards kinship were it confined to simple matter of fact, devoid of sentiment and imagination.

I know absolutely nothing about meteorological science ; but I watch the weather daily, and am just now extremely puzzled why the authorities on the subject go on predicting in the papers, day after day, for this district, "some rain, thunder locally," "rainy," etc., for the last three weeks, whereas we have been as dry as a lime-burner's wig the whole time ; the wind blowing cold and dry all the same, whether from north, west, or south.

Q

I also wonder whether any of these experts remark the extraordinary white glare that surrounds the sun, and which has more or less done so since the year 1883. My brother Robert, who is a very keen observer of the heavens, has long noticed this phenomenon, and he wrote to Mr. Ruskin in the winter of 1884 on the subject.

In London possibly it would not be so easily observed on account of the smoke and small space of sky visible between the tall houses. Town-dwellers, so long as the sun shines, are comparatively independent of the weather, as water-carts lay the dust, greengrocers supply the vegetables, butchers and poulterers the meat, and so on ; importation from abroad, and the vast system of railways, neutralising the effects of local drought. But when you come to live in the country you soon learn to give its true value to every drop of rain, and note with anxiety the entire stoppage to vegetation which spring drought occasions. Here, in Berkshire, this spring,

the outlook for the farmers is piteous in the
extreme : hay has already gone up £1 a ton ;
the young corn and root crops scarcely show
in the parched-up fields ; the springs on the
downs are again running dry, water having
to be fetched at great trouble and expense
from a distance of four miles, so that farmers
have the greatest trouble to find food and
drink for their live stock.

I am one of Her Majesty's Commissioners
for Income Tax, and last week sat in our old
Town Hall hearing appeals, chiefly from
farmers. It was heart-breaking work to go
through the accounts, one after another, of
these old farmers ; men with grand weather-
beaten faces recounting their losses in broad
Saxon dialect. Small farmers seemed to have
suffered most ; but all are in a very bad way
in the matter of profit. Many farmers about
here are giving up their tenancies, whilst
others simply keep on their farms in working
order in hopes of better times. The reason
for the depopulation of our villages is not

far to seek. Agriculture has almost ceased to pay its cost; our lanes swarm with tramps and our towns with the unemployed.

One little crumb of comfort the drought affords, which is, that the dry, dusty state of the soil facilitates the extraction, by the rake-harrow, of the baneful couch grass. On every side you see around here heaps of this wiry - looking weed scratched up and burning in small bonfires.

You, dear Marco, unlike the son of Zippor, summoned me, in your last letter, to bless; and I, unlike the son of Beor, have in response given nothing but dismal utterances. You ask for a more cheerful letter, and when the long-wished-for rain has come I will gladly accede to your desire. My flowers and garden shall be my theme, and I promise to banish entirely the depression and gloom which has latterly pervaded my letters.

G. D. L.

LETTER XXXIV

11*th July* 1892.

DEAR MARCO—I have just returned from
a short visit to Bremen, where I have placed
my second boy, Jack, to learn German and
business ways.   I went over there, *viâ* Southampton, in the North German steamship
Aller, a large Atlantic boat.   We were long
in crossing,—two whole days,—owing to
fog, which, soon after starting, came on very
densely.   We could only creep along, sound-
ing the fog-horn every three minutes ; and, as
it was, we narrowly escaped running down a
small schooner in the channel.   Our engines

were suddenly reversed, and only just in time, as the schooner went past us with but six or seven feet to spare, the crew on the deck being all ready to jump overboard.

Bremen is a picturesque old place, at least its old parts, and of course I saw Roland and

Small Farm-house near Bremen.

the Rathskeller, with the Lady Rose and Twelve Apostles, as the huge vats of wine are called ; but the more interesting sights to me were those I saw in the country, at a friend's house a short distance from the town. The ground is flat and very sandy, but full of picturesque details. I saw a large cottage

with a stork's nest on its thatched roof, with
the old storks and four young ones ; the birds
showing very conspicuously against the sky.
The cottages, which are like my sketch, are
very large ; the barn, or storehouse, and the
dwelling-places being all included under one
large roof, on the top of which the storks
build.

The peasant dwells with his family below,
where are also his stables, whilst in large lofts
above are stored the hay, etc.   The walls are
whitewashed, and the doors and window-
frames are kept brightly painted with green ;
the whole looking very like the toy houses
we get from Germany.

The enterprising Bremeners have lately
made a ship-canal, to take the place of the
tortuous windings of the river Weser.   The
old bed of this in places is now almost dry,
and one such place was close to where I was
staying.   It was all alive with birds of every
sort : hooded crows, storks, gulls, plovers,
terns, sandpipers, etc.   These birds were very

tame, and wheeled and flew around, screaming
and piping all manner of lays. The whole
scene was very Dutch in character ; and with
the birds, the cows, and the evening glow,
was exceedingly paintable. Here and there
were pools of water and a few quaint old
wooden foot-bridges that would greatly have
delighted you and tempted you to many a
water-colour. The cottage walls with the
evening light on them were, I can assure you,
lighter than the sky, as were also the gulls
and the white on the cows. It was very Cuyp-
like in effect.

In my garden I have some teasels which
are just coming into bloom. Their water-
cups were never empty, even during the very
dry weather we had. I have heard it said
that the water in these cups is sweetish in
order to attract flies, but I am rather doubtful
as to this. I cannot detect any sweetness in
the water that is found on my teasels. As
the plant is sometimes infested by aphidæ or
green flies, it is possible that the juices of

these creatures get washed down into the cups, giving it a sweetish taste. Certainly small flies do get drowned in the water at times; but I am doubtful whether the plant can be considered as a carnivorous one.

If Walter is troubled with ants or wood-lice in his hot-houses, I shall be very pleased to send him a live toad or two. Mine are very useful in this way, and live through the winter very comfortably, coming out of their holes directly the sun gains power in March. My toads alter their colour a good deal. I suppose the chameleon's alteration is somewhat of a similar character. Some days they look much darker than on others, and vary from dark gray and olive gray to light yellowish gray and ferruginous gray. I do not know whether there is anything in the somewhat similar method that toads and thrushes adopt in catching their prey that accounts for their colouring being much the same; both having olive gray backs and

yellowish speckled bellies, as well as exceedingly fine eyes.

There is a very interesting old church at
North Stoke, about two miles from here, on
the Oxfordshire side of the river, which has
hitherto entirely escaped the hands of the
restorer. It is chiefly of fourteenth century
work, the chancel, arch, and windows being
particularly beautiful and perfect; but what
I like about it is the good example it
presents of an old-fashioned English country
church of the *last* century. Here we still
have a number of old high deal pews;
quadrangular family ones of the time of
Queen Anne; a pulpit of a rather earlier
period, of oak, with the delicious bloom of
age on its surface; massive beams and ties
in the roof, probably of oak, but whitewashed
over, as are also the walls, as a matter of
course. The floor is a delightful mixture of
red tiles and bricks with flat tombstone slabs
here and there. The Royal Arms are still
in their place over the chancel arch, and the

ten commandments above the altar. As these sort of churches are fast becoming as extinct as the dodo, through the restless

Old Sun-dial on North Stoke Church.

activity of clergymen and architects, it is consoling to know that utter absence of funds will save this one for a long time yet. The church stands a short way back from the river,

on slightly rising ground. The north and
east sides of the churchyard abut on a very
picturesque farmyard and out-buildings. The
tower is square, and of brick, probably
eighteenth century work, but capitally pro-
portioned, and adding greatly to the beauty of
the landscape from many points. There are
two sundials on the walls: one modern, on an
angle of the tower ; and the other, much older,
on the south wall of the aisle. I send you a
sketch of this latter, as it is rather quaint and
peculiar. The dial—a circle—is clasped to
the wall in the arms of some man or angel ;
though, if the latter, I can see no trace of
wings. I fancy I can make out on the top half
of the dial an A and Ω, but the Ω is a little
doubtful. The other sketches I enclose are
from some mural decorations which have been
discovered on the south wall of the aisle,
behind the pulpit. The whole wall seems to
have been decorated at some time. There is
a small frieze of figure subjects divided by
lines and scroll work along the upper part,

and beneath are a number of figures of saints,
etc., designed on a much larger scale. My
sketches are from the smaller frieze, which
seemed to represent the martyrdom of some
saints by paynims or heathens. In one is

From a Wall Painting at North Stoke Church.

seen a saint dragged before a ruler; in the
other are two figures, probably representing
executioners, which form part of a procession,
two saints being prisoners. The faces of the
heathen have dark complexions and hideous
features; the martyrs having pale faces. One
of these executioners carries a curious-looking

axe, and the other what looks like a pot of
fire. The whole of the designs are executed
in pale blue and dark Indian red; at least, very
little other colour is used, as far as I can see.
There seems to have been little attempt to

Executioners from a Wall Painting at North Stoke Church.

rule the bordering lines which divide the subjects, as they are by no means true or square.
The whole is done in a very free and bold
style, which gives it a pleasant look.

In our own parish church of St. Leonard's
there are two beautiful arches in the chancel
with very fine Norman work on them of

about the time of Henry II. I daresay you
remember them ; but I do not think I called
your attention to the decoration of the bordering of one of the capitals, evidently meant
for interlacing chain-mail, which was intro-

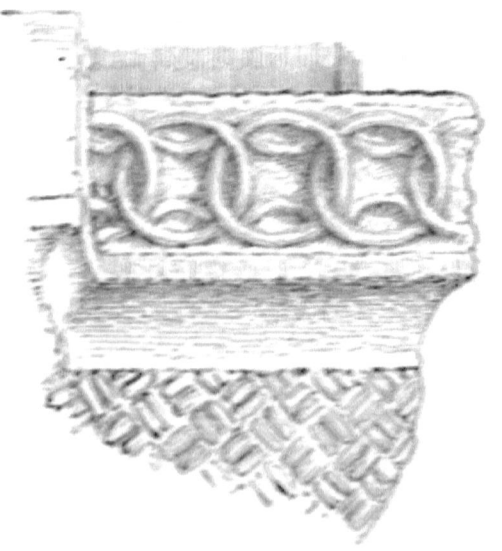

Chain-mail Moulding, St. Leonard's Church, Wallingford.

duced from the Saracens by the crusaders in
about the early part of the thirteenth century,
so I send you a sketch of it. When examin-
ing the heaps of remains, at Reading, of the
old abbey, I came across precisely the same
moulding.   G. D. L.

LETTER XXXV

15th August 1892.

DEAR MARCO—In travelling lately by railway during the very dry weather, I could
not help noticing the destruction caused by
sparks from the engine amongst grass,
weeds, and hedges on the banks at the sides.
On the Great Western the banks are generally bordered by a quickset hedge and
posts and rails. The hedge in dry, hot
weather catches fire very easily, and men
have sometimes to be placed along the
line to watch the hedge, in order to whip
out the flames and prevent them spreading
through to the standing corn. In many
places one sees burnt patches and gaps, the

results of fire. I have found out, however, from repeated observation, that there is one plant which seems to be almost incombustible : it is the wild clematis, or "traveller's joy." Wherever there are patches of this pretty straggling plant it remains bright and green, even in the midst of surrounding conflagration. Large masses of this climber grow on the chalk banks of the line as it approaches Basingstoke; and indeed it is very plentiful anywhere on the Great Western between Reading and Swindon. It is an instance of the survival of the fittest ; and I am quite sure if it were encouraged to grow well over and amongst the hedges and banks it would save the company much trouble and expense, besides adding to the beauty of the banks.

Though there is much that is extremely interesting in the theories of the evolutionists on the fertilisation of plants by bees and insects, much still remains to be accounted for, and many facts seem to contradict their

R

arguments.   I alluded to the apparently un-
accountable fertilisation of the fig and the
butcher's broom in a former letter : there are
no attractions of gaudy bloom or honey here
to draw the bees or flies.   And as to the
colour and beauty of flowers being intended
to serve for the perpetuation of the species,
how is it that the ivy, white clover, migno-
nette, and a host of other inconspicuous flowers
draw more bees and flies round them than
many brighter and showily coloured plants
do.   I do not believe the beauty of the plant
has much to do with it ; for bees and flies,
unless I have been misinformed, have exceedingly short sights, their eyes being made with
great magnifying power and adapted solely
for close-inspection work.   It seems to me,
they must be guided by their scent instinct,
whatever that may be : the same instinct
that leads them to the flowers teaches them
the way back to their hives.   What I want
to fight for is the beauty of the flower.   I do
not want to have any use attached to it,

except the glory of the Creator and the
delight of eyes capable of seeing that glory.
Mere perpetuation of species could be at-
tained easily without all this elaborate display
of beauty.   I also hold with Mr. Ruskin that
the blossom is the culminating glory and perfection of a plant's life.   All further ripening
of seed being effected during the plant's
decadence, and with a view to a further display in following years.

The plant's usefulness is quite another
question.   As far as the plant is concerned,
the said usefulness does not always prove an
advantage, but on the contrary often causes
its destruction.   Many food-supplying plants
would very soon get exterminated were they
not carefully preserved and cultivated by
man.

G. D. L.

LETTER XXXVI

22nd August 1892.

DEAR MARCO—Our mutual friend, Dr.
Buzzard, once expressed his surprise to me
that, fond as I am of plants and their ways
of growth and beauty, I should never have
taken up botany as a serious study. The fact
is, I am, I think, too fond of flowers to do
so; I could never get myself to associate
these beautiful objects of creation in any way
with the dry nomenclature and everlasting
classification with which botanical science
seems to me to be overladen.

There are plenty of available books on
flowers, of a popular character, written for

children, ladies, and lazy people like myself,
which, with a slight modicum of scientific
knowledge, personal observation, and the
help of good illustrations, serve well enough
to teach one to recognise and name any plant
that may be met with in our own country,
without giving the trouble and time necessary
to master the deeper mysteries of the science.

The worst, however, of these books is that
so very little that is really interesting on the
subject of plants is afforded by them : most
of these sort of popular works being rendered
obnoxious to one by the vast amount of
superfluous padding that is worked into them ;
such, for instance, as pretty sentiments on
the happy years of childhood, rural felicity,
spring's delights, together with numerous
quotations from the poets. This "harmless
and blameless and free from all goodness"
style is, to those who regard God's handiwork
with the wonder and reverence it demands,
nearly as repulsive as the facetious tone
assumed by many writers of popular works

on natural history for boys, who, for instance, in describing the ways of a frog, playfully call it "froggy," whilst a mole is "the little gentleman in black."

There are, however, some first-rate popular works on flowers and botany : Mr. Robinson's *English Flower Garden*, and the Rev. C. T. John's *Flowers of the Field* being very notable examples ; but even in the last-named work space necessarily prevents the introduction of much about the plants which one would like to know. The descriptions of the plants, though correct enough, are not nearly so graphic and interesting as those to be found in Gerard or Parkinson, written nearly three hundred years before. Take, for example, the description of the fig-wort. In the modern work :

Scrophularia nodosa (Knotted Fig-wort).—Stem square, with angles blunt ; leaves smooth, heart-shaped, tapering to a point ; flowers in loose panicles.   Moist bushy places ; common.   A tall herbaceous plant, 3-4 feet high, with repeatedly forked panicles of almost globular dingy purple flowers, but attractive neither in form nor colour.   Fl. June,

July, Per. (name from the disease for which the plant was
formerly thought a specific).

All this is practical enough, and no doubt
satisfactorily correct ; but hear how J. Gerard
describes it :

Of great Figgewoort, or Kernell woort. *Scrophularia
major*.   Great Figwoort.

THE DESCRIPTION.

The great Figgewoort springeth up with stalks fower
square two cubites high, of a dark purple colour, and hollow
within : the leaves growe alwaies by couples, as it were
from one joint, opposite or standing one right against the
other, broad, sharp-pointed, snipped rounde about the edges
like the leaves of the greater nettle, but bigger, blacker, and
nothing at all stinging when they be touched : the flowers
in the tops of the branches are of a dark purple colour, very
like in forme to little helmets : there commeth up little small
seede in pretic rounde buttons, but sharpe at the ends : the
roote is whitish, beset with little knobs and bunches as it
were knots and kirnals.

THE PLACE.

The great Scrophularia groweth plentifully in shadowie
woods, and sometimes in moist meadows, especially in
greatest abundance in a woode as you go from London to
Hornesey, and also in Stowe woode, and Shotover neere
Oxenforde.

Gerard still believes in the virtues of the
plant, and appends useful receipts, whereas,
though the modern botanists probably no
longer believe in the virtues of the plant,
they still retain its repulsive Latin name.
Gerard's book is of great use in determining
and explaining the meaning of the old English
names that are still used for many of our
plants ; as, for instance, in the apparently odd
name for a rather rare water plant, "the
water violet" (*Hottonia palustris*), the bloom
of which is not in the least like the ordinary
violet either in shape or growth.   This plant
is really of the primrose family ; but the
blossom grows somewhat in the manner of
the stocks of our garden, which in Gerard are
often termed violets, as well as are the gilly-
flowers.   It is no doubt on account of the
resemblance of the flowers that the name
originated.   Gerard describes the flowers of
the water violet as "like unto Stocke Gilloflowers, with some yellownesse in the middle."
This confusion of nomenclature is thus further

explained in his chapter 298 on violets, which,
as it is very expressive and characteristic, I
cannot refrain from sending to you at length :

There might be described many kinds of flowers under
this name of violets, if the differences should be more curiously looked into than is necessorie : for we might joine
heereunto the Stock Gilloflowers, the Wall Flowers, Dame's
Gilloflowers, Marian's Violets, and likewise some of the
bulbed Flowers, bicause some of them by Theophrastus are
termed Violets. But this was not our charge, holding it
sufficient to distinguish and divide them as neere as may be
in kindred and neighbourhood ; addressing myselfe unto the
Violets called the blacke or purple Violets, or March Violets
of the Garden, which have a great prerogative above others,
not only bicause the minde conceiveth a certain pleasure
and recreation by smelling and handling of these most
odoriferous flowers, but also for that very many by these
Violets receive ornament and comely grace : for there be
made of them Garlands for the heade, nosgaies and poesies,
which are delightfull to looke on and pleasant to smell to,
speaking nothing of their appropriate vertues ; yea, Gardens
themselves receive by these the greatest ornaments of all,
cheifest beautie, and most gallant grace ; and the recreation
of the minde which is taken heereby, cannot be but verie
good and honest : for they admonish and stir up a man to
that which is comely and honest ; for flowers through their
beautie, varietie of colour, and exquisite forme, do bring to
a liberall and gentle manly minde, the remembrance of

honestie, comelinesse, and all kinds of vertues.   For it
would be an unseemely and filthie thing, as a certaine wise
man saith, for him that doth looke upon and handle fair and
beautifull things, and who frequenteth and is conversant in
faire and beautifull places, to have his minde not faire but
filthie and deformed ?

Gerard gives the Latin name of the water
violet, *Viola palustris*, which at any rate is
pretty, if a little misleading ; and I confess I
do not see that " Hottonia," which is derived
from a botanist's name, is a bit more appropriate to the plant.

Gerard's book would be quite satisfactory
enough for any one of my disposition, were it
not so very large and cumbersome, and rather
badly indexed.   The illustrations, though
rough, are generally very accurate and fine
specimens of the art of woodcutting of the
period.

G. D. L.

LETTER XXXVII

6th March 1893.

DEAR MARCO—Last week Mrs. Leslie and
I stayed for a few days at a friend's house up
on the hills at Ipsden, about four miles from
here. There are very extensive woods all
along the range of hills which are known as
the Chilterns, and which lie exactly between
Wallingford and Henley.   Here there is a
large estate, consisting chiefly of woodland,
belonging to the mother of the gentleman at
whose house we stayed, of which he has the
entire care and management.   I here had an
opportunity of learning a little about forestry
and the felling of trees, which was entirely a

new subject to me. My friend does wonders
amongst the trees by judicious thinning,
pruning, etc. ; and I was quite surprised to
find what large profits could be made out of
such woods by careful and intelligent treat-
ment. A plantation of trees properly looked
after is not nearly so picturesque as one that
is neglected, but the difference in value and
usefulness is immense. What is called a
"fall" or cutting of timber for sale, in a well-
managed wood, can be taken nearly every
three or four years, and as the trimmings and
faggots pay for the labour, the profit on well-
grown timber is pretty large. If, however, the
woods are badly looked after, the trees grow
thick and drawn up, many inferior sorts
stunting and destroying the better ones ; and
when a fall is taken great destruction and
waste occurs owing to the crowded state of
the growth, and very few young trees are
found of sufficient strength to take the place
of the old ones.

We saw a fine large beech tree brought

down. The whole operation was very simple, and occupied somewhat less than a quarter of an hour. Two old men and one old woman did it ; none of them grand in any way, in fact they were very short in stature. One of these men first cut neatly through the spreading root-tops at the base of the stem of the tree, making perfectly clean notches in them all round with a very sharp axe, which seemed to go through the beechwood as if it were only cheese. Then what they called the fall was made ; this was a larger and deeper notch on the side the tree was intended to fall. It requires some knowledge to select where a tree should fall, so as to do least damage to its neighbours. Many young tall saplings are hooked back with hooks on the end of long poles, so as to make way for the fall. The tree we saw brought down had a strong natural list to the south ; but by the proper placement of the fall-notch, the tree was eventually brought down due west. When the fall had been carefully cut with the axe, a long, narrow saw was worked through the stem, one man holding the saw handle at its base and the other the handle at its end, whilst the woman pulled at a small rope attached to the saw, which greatly accelerated the forward cut. An iron wedge was after a bit inserted opposite to the fall; and in a very few minutes, with very little preliminary warning, down came the sixty-foot tree, exactly in the place intended for it. The cubic measurement of the tree was then marked with the axe on the stem. The woman, I was told, was a most invaluable person; not only looking after the men's dinners, etc., but being extremely dexterous in chopping up faggots and brushwood, and doing a lot of work. It looked as if it would be utterly impossible for the tree to fall in the direction it did.

There is, very near Well Place, where we were staying, an old disused well, said to be the work of the Romans, now dry and

much overgown by brushwood; and I was
told that some years ago a wretched woman
threw her six months' old baby down this,
expecting, of course, that it would be killed
and its dead body probably not found for a
long time.   It happened, however, a day and
a half after the child had been thrown in, that
some passers-by, hearing a cry from the well,
had it searched with great difficulty, when the
baby was found and brought up very little
injured, and eventually lived for seven or
eight years.   It was supposed that the child's
dress must have acted somewhat as a para-
chute in the confined air of the shaft of the
well, and so broken the fall.

I have not much to tell you in the bird
line since my last letter, except that some
sand-martins built their nest in a drain-pipe,
or what builders term a weeper, in the high
retaining wall at the approach to my boat-
house.   This wall rises from the river some
twelve feet or more, and the weepers in it are
to allow the water from the bank behind it to

escape.   There are several of them in the
wall, and as they are just the size of the sand-
martins' nest - holes, the birds selected the
place as one suitable and ready made for their
purpose.

Lots of these sand-martins collect with the
other swallows over the river, in September,
prior to leaving.   We always have plenty of
swifts here.   I picked up a dead one once
and measured its wings spread out.   It was
eighteen inches; it seems an enormous width.

In a very pretty little book called *A Year
with the Birds*, written by an Oxford tutor,
I found a note as to the hovering of the kingfisher, which seems to have some bearing on
the evolutions of this bird, which I described
in a former letter to you.   The author says :
" I have seen a kingfisher hovering like a
dragon-fly or humming-bird over a little sap-
ling almost underneath the bridge by which
you enter Addison's Walk.   Possibly it was
about to strike a fish, but unluckily it saw me
and vanished.   The sight was one of mar-

vellous beauty, though it lasted but a few seconds."

A kingfisher frequents the inside of my boat-house every year in the winter months, evidently, by his marks, sitting on the edge of my punt; and once or twice on going down the steps to look at the boats the bird has flown out through the entrance-way, so close over my head that I could have caught it easily with my hand if I had not been so startled.

On looking through my letters to you I find I have left unsaid very much that would have interested you, especially as regards the plants and flowers in my garden. Flowers, however, must be seen growing *in situ* to enjoy them properly. Descriptions of their beauty are of very little value; even the pleasure derived from cut flowers, as decorations for our rooms, is as nothing to that which is felt by those who plant, nurture, and watch their growth from bud to seed-time.

Your son Walter has all this pleasure in

s

the little hot-houses he has constructed in
your town garden.   Horticulture is, I am sure,
when really personally attended, one of the
most refining and interesting hobbies a man
is capable of enjoying.   I sometimes wish my
garden were not so large ; for, as I do all the
flower part of it myself, I can scarcely find
time to do it justice.   In town gardens the
great difficulty is to get things to grow ; but
in the country things grow only too fast and
too thick, and one's whole time is taken up
by preventing the spread of the clumps one
into another in inextricable confusion.   Plants,
when first introduced, seem small, but in a
very few years they overspread their original
space and have to be taken up and divided ;
thus in the autumn I feel dreadfully cruel and
wasteful in absolutely throwing on the rubbish-
heap strong roots and clumps of such things
as the day - lilies, German irises, Japanese
anemones, antirrhinums, Iceland poppies,
globe-thistles, doronicums, aconites, etc.   Of
course there must be some people who would

be glad of such things, and if they would in the autumn come and pack them up and take them away I should be only too thankful ; but I am too lazy to do this packing and the necessary letter-writing myself.

As I write, my crocuses and scillas are blazing out in the warm sun, surrounded by swarms of bees: a spring burst of glory that is most exhilarating; and with the cheerful and hopeful feelings inspired by it, I will say farewell to my dear Marco.

G. D. L.

THE END

Printed by R. & R. Clark, *Edinburgh.*